FEBRUARY 2021 - ISSUE 173

FICTION

NON-FICTION

Neil Clarke: Publisher/Editor-in-Chief
Sean Wallace: Editor
Kate Baker: Non-Fiction Editor/Podcast Director

Clarkesworld Magazine (ISSN: 1937-7843) • Issue 173 • February 2021

www.clarkesworldmagazine.com

The Failed Dianas

MONIQUE LABAN

The hostess adjusts her glasses when I repeat my name and reservation time.

"Of course," she says. "We've switched you from the balcony seating to the chef's table. We hope you don't mind."

I follow her past the bar and four-tops to the back of the restaurant, where a row of line cooks mince parsley and knead dough. Beyond the dough's malty sweetness, I take in the rich smell of roast geese as they're basted by the sous chef and bananas caramelizing deeper into the kitchen. I cover my nose to keep myself from getting nauseous once I'm seated at the end of the counter, away from the other customers. When a waiter slips a basket of rolls at my elbow, I break one open and let the steam wash over my face.

The internship supervisor warned me that eighteen hours is the standard length of time I should wait once back on Earth before exposing myself to strong aromas and tastes. It's the second time I've broken that rule in as many trips back from the C. P. Menlo Cosmocurrencies Division. Nothing happened the first time, but I don't want to risk throwing up tonight. The line cooks stare like the hostess did, tighten their smiles, and make a show of complimenting each other on their prep work. The sommelier pops by to ask if I'd like their house recommendation. It occurs to me that this may be the only spot in Pittsburgh that won't card me.

"Whatever pairs well with bread rolls," I say.

"Excellent choice," says the sommelier.

With half an hour left before closing time, I had expected the restaurant to clear out so that I could have more privacy with the original Diana, but the bar is full and several booths are celebrating various occasions. I look for Diana when a holographic birthday dessert bursts open at a long table, and again when waitstaff claps for a woman proposing to her longtime partner, and a third time when the hostess and the sous argue over a customer's order.

When I finish my fourth helping of bread rolls, I focus on the line cooks instead, sipping white wine to block my sinuses and dull my sense of smell. I watch them as their knives flutter onions into ribbons, dash cognac into flames over steel pans. I catch a whiff of hickory smoke and search for the dish that wafts it.

"Mom and Dad never taught you how to cook, did they?" asks someone next to me. It's my voice, but huskier. I turn and see myself at twice my age.

I hate Original Diana immediately, or at least I want to hate her. Nothing should surprise me about her appearance, yet I'm embarrassed to be excited to look like her when I'm in my forties. My cheeks get hot when I think about how I held out a shred of hope that she would look, at best, like a shoddy beta version of me. Instead, her black jumpsuit and moonrock jewelry make her striking against my postflight black curls and simple skater dress. The restaurant website's proud newspaper reviews had the same glowing face, surrounded by the same chic mid-century interior and tantalizing food. I tried to convince myself that it was makeup, surgery, Photoshop, or some other conflation of the truth. But I'm here now, in her domain. Original Diana smiles at me.

"Nope," I say. "They didn't want me becoming another restaurateur."

"I figured," she responds.

Original Diana chuckles, takes a seat, and waves at the line cooks, who stand there with grins on their faces like they're the hungry ones, waiting for her to explain what the hell is going on. No two people would have looked this similar unless they were identical twins, and our age difference is clear. Diana ignores them. She reaches her hand out like a question, and I nod. She takes my chin in with the tips of her fingers and tilts my head around.

"So Mom and Dad advanced the replication technique once they got the hang of perfecting simple body parts for their hospital patients," she starts. "I'm sure they never wanted an exact duplicate of me anyway."

She notes how my nose is narrower and how I'm skinnier than she was at my age. She gasps when she realizes I don't wear contacts.

"Noticeably lighter skin, too, than either me or them. Perhaps they thought you'd be safer that way," Diana says. "Amazing what someone can do when they don't adhere to legal restrictions on cloning. What did they use?"

"They grew me from an eyelash on your pillow," I say. Her hand leaves my face, and she sips from a glass of water that the hostess has placed for her. I inhale and begin the speech I had planned. "At first, they tried fingernails, then blood, then hair. None worked and they were running out of your DNA, but they lucked out. They speed-incubated the cells from the eyelash up to when you were thirteen, so I would have a wide memory base and they would only have to worry about raising me through high school and college. It's a method that took them—"

"Thirteen years to perfect and eight years to raise you," Original Diana finishes. The calm with which she intuits the line feels like a violation, as if I'm the one who hasn't realized there's a second iteration of myself. Original Diana swivels in the barstool so that she can lean against the counter. Behind her, another birthday dessert arrives to a small family. The bartender announces last call. "They raised me for a bit longer than that, Diana. The full twenty-one years."

"But I wasn't—" I start.

"A disappointment?" Original Diana says, her lips tugging at the seams. "Yes, you're now the same age I was when I ruined things for everyone and drove my life down the gutter. I was a selfish brat who got into Pitt instead of Carnegie Mellon, switched my major from galactic finance to art history, dropped out when I was twenty-one, and haven't been seen since the screaming match with my parents about wanting to be a chef. All they ever wanted to do was look out for me when I had myopic dreams that would never take off. I was just some spoiled brat like all the white children whose parents didn't know how to raise them."

Original Diana keeps going and matches what Mom and Dad have said word for word. My mind goes blank. It's the story that my . . . *our* parents told me when they woke me at thirteen. I've heard it every birthday since.

The Original Diana never amounted to anything. Grabe naman. If only she had listened to us and gone into interstellar futures projection, like cosmocurrencies, once the cryptocurrency boom went bust. She'd have been a happy daughter rather than a hopeless ingrate with no future. Her life has been in shambles ever since she left home, a black hole sucking in the promise of a secure career.

Ruined, selfish, spoiled. When Original Diana gets to the "hopeless ingrate" part, the unnerving precision makes my throat run dry.

Don't be those things, Diana. Don't leave us like she did. We love you and want what's best for you. Please let us know if you need anything, anak. Family always stays together.

"I'm clearly doing poorly with my Michelin-starred city restaurant," Original Diana says. She leans in and whispers into my face. "I was a wild, unreasonable monster. Obviously, they should have punished me more while I was growing up."

There had always been a small fear in the back of my mind that my parents had kept something from me, but Original Diana's intent repetition of what she went through over twenty years ago confirms what I didn't want to believe was true: if they wanted to, or if I ever crossed them, Mom and Dad could be unspeakably cruel.

Original Diana's full lips spread into a broad smile, and the hush as she waits for me to react lingers until I notice that the line cooks have cleaned up their stations and the waitstaff are clustered by the bar. The last customers pay their checks and leave. Diana turns away from me for a moment to announce to her staff that she'll close up for the night. They holler back thank-yous that find middle ground between her and me.

While she has her back to me, I leap from my barstool and bolt to the emergency exit behind us. None of this is going as planned. The door leads out to a crowded alley of more staff smoking with burly strangers in employee uniforms that I recognize from the neighboring shops. They greet me as "boss" and try to pass me a cigarette. This isn't going as planned either. I excuse myself, step back into the restaurant, and shut the door.

"You forgot your bag, Diana," Original Diana calls after me. "We always forget our bag, don't we?"

I whip around.

"I had a speech," I yell at her. "I waited for the crappy bus for forty minutes to get from Carnegie Mellon to the South Side in an hour."

"Was that speech literally what I said, but with our roles reversed?" Diana states more than asks. "Remember, I know you. And no, saying it to my face is not going to make you feel better about yourself. You will always feel like a disappointment, and that's not my fault."

The shock spreads over me. *We* always forget our bag. She's done this before.

"Diana, I've gone through this with three other clones," she says. Each word scrapes at the floor of my gut. "Those thirteen years of modifying the replication process? Mom and Dad created a clone the same year I stopped contact with them. And another four years after that. And again six years after that. Each one left Mom and Dad when they were twenty-one. You're the fourth clone. The fifth Diana."

My face turns to ice and sinks along with the rest of my numb body. Original Diana stands up from her stool and wraps me in a bear hug, then leads me to a booth to sit down. The restaurant has emptied, so her voice echoes against every wall when she speaks.

"There is no version of us that will ever make our parents completely happy," she says. "There are only versions of us that have done our best to make ourselves happy."

• • •

The other Dianas arrive in their own time. Once Original Diana caught my dinner reservation, she called the others to make sure they could make it to the city by nightfall—a tradition, she explained. DeeDee, the first clone that awoke the year Original Diana left, arrives five minutes after Original Diana texts her. A crown of leaves decorates her shaved scalp in black ink.

"My tattoo shop's down the street," DeeDee says after she greets me with a high-five. She turns to Original Diana. "Remember when I first found you? I went all the way up to your fancy New York culinary school and I beat you up all cliché clone battle-style."

"You mean when you punched a tooth loose and I had to protect myself with my favorite Santoku knife?" Original Diana says. She rolls her eyes. "Nope, it never crosses my mind."

The two break into laughter and Original Diana punches DeeDee on the shoulder. DeeDee smirks and turns to me.

"I was so mad. All the time. There was so much rage in the eighteen-year-old memory Original Diana held, and I blamed it all on her. And our parents. And, well, everything. There was no way Mom and Dad would've made me be a financial analyst in the Milky Way. Not right then after they had put her through eighteen years of shit. I knew I had to escape."

The next clone, 3D, lugs in a carry-on from the red-eye transport hypertube from California, where she owns her own gym and dance studio.

"I was seventeen when I woke up and not much happier than either of them," 3D says, smoothing out her post-transport blonde hair. She asks Original Diana for any Sonoma County wines and pours us each a glass. "DeeDee was so close in age to Original Diana that all our parents had to do was accuse people of playing into the racist stereotype of all Asians looking the same if anyone got suspicious about illegal replication and advanced incubation. For me, though, Mom and Dad decided to move out west to make sure no one would figure out what they were up to. I tried to get along with them when we moved to California, but it was stressful for us all to adjust to a new place. On top of that, I had to deal with their usual manipulation and abuse."

I flinch at the word "abuse." It's a word for other people, never one that I feel ever applied to me. It still doesn't, but there are three other versions of me who look down when it's mentioned.

"3D was the first Diana to make it to space," Original Diana says. "It broke our parents' hearts that she never wanted to go back up again.

She got tons of funding to study abroad in the lunar colony, and she couldn't stand it."

"Hypertubes are the only way I travel now," 3D continues. "I did Pilates constantly when I was on the moon, and even then, I came back so sore and claustrophobic from the compact housing that I begged Mom and Dad to compromise. Leave behind my interstellar economics major with an MLS degree so I could be lab techs like them and actually help people for a living."

My shoulders tighten thinking about those cramped hallways at the Cosmocurrencies Division and their dim gray lights. Their vacuum-packed blankness, their shrink-wrap surfaces. 3D slides next to me and kneads the base of my neck until my shoulders relax.

"Obviously, I wasn't allowed to switch majors since—"

"You can help whoever and do whatever you want wherever you want once you have a seven-figure interstellar trader salary," Original Diana and DeeDee finish in unison.

Dr. Diana, the fourth one, arrives an hour after we're halfway through our second glasses of wine. Doc was awakened at age fifteen and now lives in Brooklyn, where she teaches animation at the School of Visual Arts.

"Space was absolutely colorless," Doc mentions. "I spent so much time up there reading comic books and doodling all over my antigravity pod in dry erase markers for fun. I failed my basic interstellar upkeep class on purpose so that Mom and Dad would worry that I wouldn't even be able to survive up there."

"They're not so bad anymore," I say, and Doc nods. The other three Dianas don't. Doc reaches across the table and holds my hand.

"Honestly, it seems that they've chilled out quite a bit," Doc says. "Sure, they still screamed at me and called me a failure every now and then, but from fifteen to twenty-one it was as if they were more worried about losing another daughter."

"And all they had to do was go back far enough into their own kid's memory to make sure they hadn't messed her up at whatever age yet, it's totally fine," DeeDee mocks. "Way easier than, say, not punishing their kid for wanting to live her own life."

"They're in their seventies now," I argue. "They were hoping to have retired a few years back. They don't raise their voices at me, only when Original Diana is brought up. I could be their last chance for them to have a daughter who provides financial and emotional stability for them."

None of the Dianas nod this time. Instead, Original Diana reminds me that it was because of her that our parents barred me from the kitchen when they prepared meals. She sent them the nail from her middle finger, a sprig of mint from one of her early dishes stuck in its arc.

DeeDee sent a bandage covered in the blood that seeped out of her first sleeve, and her attitude meant that our parents took me to therapy as soon as I woke up at thirteen. 3D's hair had been covered with sweat from a wellness retreat she hosted, and our parents had kept me from enrolling in athletics and dance classes when they found such a strong affection for it in my memory. Doc's eyelash fell on one of her storyboards, not a pillowcase, and still had ink stuck on it when she mailed it to our parents. They kept me from watching cartoons and reading comic books under the reasoning that I was "too old" for them at thirteen. I hadn't come from one Diana. I had come from a line of them, each replicated from the previous version.

"Each time we mail a piece of ourselves to Mom and Dad to give them a chance to repeat the replication process, we also add a letter and a check," Original Diana says. "The letter explains that they can use our DNA, or they can process the check. Not both. We all pool however much we can live without into the check, and the amount reflects how successful we've been. They can treat the money as an acceptance of how we live our lives, and we'll know we can start contact again. Last time, eight years ago, that amount hit over half a million dollars. We're doing pretty well."

All the other Dianas stare at me as Original Diana continues.

"In the three times we've done this, Mom and Dad have never once processed the check," she says. She shifts in her seat and rests her head in her hand. The other Dianas see this as a cue to lean back. "But all that aside, let's get to know you, Diana. How do you feel about your internship in cosmocurrencies? Or we can cut to the point. Why did you come here, now?"

I'm a solid seventeen hours postflight, but it's as if my throat and my head have decided to battle each other with nausea and fear. I tell them about my first week of orientation, how C. P. Menlo expects its interns to abide by ten-hour days, and how easily those ten hours turned into eleven, twelve, fourteen. The competitive nature of the interns who wanted to be hired at the end of the trial program meant I often didn't socialize. I kept to myself to prevent them from sabotaging me like they did to each other. The whole Division was largely devoid of any sensory stimuli. It kept us focused on its endless spreadsheets and formulae, but it couldn't keep the smell of space out.

"It was like seared steak and diesel fumes wherever I went," I say when DeeDee asks. 3D and Doc chew on their lips. "It's not something that anyone else picked up on. No one could do anything about it anyway, even if I complained to HR. I couldn't get away from the stench. I ran into the nearest Sephora as soon as orientation was over and I was back on Earth."

I dropped a third of my intern wages on the bottles of perfume I could carry in my luggage back to campus, where I sat in my dorm in an oakmoss and bergamot and tonka bean haze, layering one after another until I forgot about that steak-and-diesel smell, that internship, and the career that I would be stuck in for the rest of my working life.

The next time I went back up, I brought sample vials from a specialty boutique that the owner recommended. The first turned out to be a ripe rose mixed with citrus and labdanum. I let it be a surprise and spent the morning searching the Division for a rose garden. I cried at my desk once I realized the scent came from me, having warmed the fragrance on my skin with all my running around. The same thing happened when I wore a jammy spruce tree sample the following day. Every department head noticed and complimented me on the scent, earning me dirty looks from the other interns.

I spent each lunch break searching for classes, programs, degrees, ateliers, and apprenticeships. I hit my max on lunar colony library books with anything they had on the science and history of perfume. I lost sleep on fragrance community forums over how we had discovered parts of our galaxy that smell entirely of raspberries and others that smell like rum, and how we'll never venture far enough to sniff them. In spare moments in my pod, I found that not only do fragrances induce memories, but their inherent ability to replicate the things I wanted to see and feel and experience was the most alluring prospect of all, one that tipped perfume from a fascination to an obsession.

"I'm due to fly out there again next week, but I can't see myself ever going back," I say. I turn to Original Diana. "You were right when you asked if I was here to see if I could use your failure as leverage to let Mom and Dad know that I'd turn out better. I wanted to learn why you made them so miserable for not doing what they wanted. I've never disobeyed them."

The rest of the Dianas are silent as the Original Diana takes my face in her hand again. They must know what I've been doing. They must know how this feels.

"You've been researching how to make perfume," she says, and this is when my tears come. "You've kept this from them to protect yourself. Diana, no one gets to promise anyone else their life simply because of some pathetic attempt to justify having brought them into existence."

I think back to my floating closet of an office and the colorless mornings when I walked mechanically to my desk, pretending to myself that I had engine fluid instead of blood in my veins so that I could trick myself into being nothing more than a number-crunching robot for the next ten hours or so.

There have been fewer perfumers in the history of the world than there had been astronauts in this year alone. I had been clinging to this fact like maybe it would soften our parents to my side, but I know, and the other Dianas know, that this will not save me. Perfume is the only thing I've wanted that hasn't been tied to whether Mom and Dad wanted it, too.

"I have three semesters before graduation. It's just enough time and overlapping credits to slip in a chemistry major to meet the minimum requirements for most master's programs in scent design. I've been scheduling informational interviews with top perfume schools," I say. "There's nothing like it and I've never felt like I've used my time so meaningfully before."

The other Dianas bow or tilt their heads in their own ways, the same grin on all their lips.

"There are so many versions of us in which we try our best to be happy," Original Diana says. "We've found at least four ways to be happy. Looks like you've found one, too."

"Let me teach you how to cook," Original Diana says. "And you can show me how to smell."

My phone keeps buzzing with emails from my internship supervisor and the C. P. Menlo human resources department to ask if I'm absolutely sure that I'm giving up my spot in the cosmocurrencies internship program. DeeDee giggles every time they send another reply *just to make sure*. Doc writes up the letter we'll be mailing to our parents, only a check and no DNA this time. We will wait and see. 3D pulls out the veggies from the industrial fridge she wants Original Diana and I to work with for our late-night dinner party, but Original Diana tells her to hold off and walks me deeper into the kitchen. I overhear them talking about their children, their partners, the new friends they've made, the places they've traveled to, and everything in between that they've been up to since they all last saw each other. I can't help but wonder what I'll end up like at twenty-nine, thirty-five, thirty-nine, and forty-two.

Original Diana takes me to where the spices and loose-leaf teas are kept, then the rooftop herb garden, then the bags of wood chips the restaurant keeps for the smoker. When I choose a handful from each area she shows me, Original Diana and I bring them back to the others and tell them to breathe in deeply.

Our breaths all match for a few seconds, and in those moments, I feel no expectations, only trust.

ABOUT THE AUTHOR

Monique Laban is a writer from New York. Her fiction has appeared in *Tiny Nightmares: Very Short Stories of Horror.* Her nonfiction has appeared in *Catapult* and *Electric Literature.* She can be summoned with comfortable midcentury furniture and particularly grisly tales of revenge.

Terra Rasa

ANASTASIA BOOKREYEVA, TRANSLATED BY RAY NAYLER

The train hurled along at such speed my ears kept popping. We rushed through Voronezh in minutes. More accurately—through what was left of Voronezh. Where there had been a river, there was an empty trough. The fire had burned away the flesh of humanity here and retreated—for a time.

Back when trains went slower, I loved looking out the window at the villages—the houses with their yellow windows, the forests and fields. Boring, sure—but this was my country, after all. I especially liked the railroad that ran along the foot of the Caucasus Mountains, the trains to Sochi rushing to the sea and back.

Now there was no more railway—and no more Sochi. Sometimes it seemed the mountains were gone as well.

Despite the air conditioning, it was so hot you wanted to strip down to indecency. At the depot the trains were sprayed down with flame-retardant solution. But that wasn't enough. They also had to be hosed down periodically with non-potable water from tanks stationed along the rails.

The train was supposed to be full, but in fact there were many empty seats. Across from me in my compartment sat a grandmother with her granddaughter. Next to her was a fat man in a tie and long-sleeved dress shirt. I still remember his sweaty face. News reports flashed across the television at random. The grandmother sat nervously. And then there was the priest in the upper berth—as grim as the latest weather forecasts. Toward evening, he began singing psalms.

The grandmother had one of those faces that told you at any moment she might pull smoked chicken, boiled eggs, and a pickle out of her pocket. I was almost drooling just thinking about it. Luckily, she didn't do anything of the kind: I don't know what I would have done if she had.

"Are you headed to Murmansk?" she asked, as if there were other options.

"Yes. To the bay."

All the ships were leaving from there, headed for the pole. As she well knew, of course. The only question anyone was asking was how to get there. People didn't think about anything else—about food or a roof over their heads. All they thought of was of something to drink. Up there was snow, ice—and that meant salvation. The problem was, there were practically no ships left.

"Where are you from?" I asked.

"From Saratov."

Saratov, Volgograd, and everything around them had burned first.

"Do you have money?"

"Burnt."

In truth, there was practically no money left in the world. A world without money. What could be better? Maybe we'd ended up in heaven and just didn't realize it yet.

I decided not to ask about the parents of the child sitting in front of me, frozen in a doll-like pose.

"I've seen so much sorrow. I've seen everything: War, and hunger. But nothing like this," Grandma said.

"Exactly right," said the priest. "This was visited upon us for a reason."

Great. Now it would start—the talk about anger from on high, about the end of the world and all that. This was the crap that had driven my boss crazy right at the beginning of it all. It came into his head one hot morning that we all needed to confess. He forced everyone to run off to church. The next day, the church burned.

I have no idea what happened to my boss. The evacuation took place, as usual, in total confusion.

"Don't talk to me about God. He's not worth praying to, if he allows all this to happen," Grandma said angrily. "And what are you doing here, I'd like to know? You should have burned up along with your flock."

I decided not to stick my nose into any religious arguments. But anyway, it was clear you don't just *end up* on this train. This was the last high-speed train from the south. All the airports had closed long ago. At first from stupidity—and then necessity. Incidentally—this grandmother and her child ending up here? Even that was some kind of miracle. But the priest?

This trip was one-way. The authorities had selflessly fled to Siberia—where, by the way, fires were also raging. Only the temperature was a little lower. That was exactly why so many people were saying God was to blame: only He, they said, could make things burn that were never meant to burn.

In my opinion, He had nothing to do with it. Whose fault was it? I had no idea. And no time to think about it, anyway.

Down at the end of the railway carriage, someone began to cry loudly. Between sobs he said, over and over, "Where is this fucking train going?"

It was clear enough where: To the end of the tunnel. But there was no light there—we were all very mistaken on that account.

"Night, street, streetlamp, pharmacy . . . " I mumbled.

All the streets, streetlamps, and pharmacies had long ago turned to ashes.

I wanted to smoke, but I'd quit when the fires started. A lot of people quit—almost everyone I knew. It was hard to hold matches or a lighter in your hand nowadays.

A dismal landscape drifted past—burned villages and forests, their outlines sketched behind the leaden wall of smoke. Scattered red blotches of flame. The fire swept in one direction and then another. After it passed, nothing was left but gray-black dust.

"Everything will be like this," I said to myself. "There's no way out . . . "

Fall came late, that year. The leaves began to fall, but without changing color. Everyone waited for winter, but it never arrived. They waited for it the following year. And then they stopped waiting. And the fires came . . .

Air conditioners disappeared from the market, and the polite girls at the electronics stores apologized.

They apologized for two weeks, while the telephone lines and electricity held out. Then the stores closed. The aquifers dried up. The lakes and rivers shrank with every passing day. A liter of drinking water was worth a fortune.

People turned primitive slowly, but irreversibly. They came to hate one another. They were prepared to commit any act of cruelty for a drop of moisture.

The more or less normal among us became volunteer rescuers—although everyone knew it was useless.

I wasn't normal, but I volunteered—and I understood the futility of it. Better to occupy your brain and your dehydrated body with *something* than to simply die of despair.

The drought and constant fires led to a shortage in food—but the lack of water was more serious. The government gave out all its reserves of food, caches the public hadn't even known about. When there's no future, why conserve any longer? Tins with unknown markings and white labels were scattered everywhere. The contents were always mushy and tasteless—but at least not rotten. Sometimes they made me nauseous, and I ate almost nothing. Only anger gave me the strength to stagger on.

The most terrifying of all the things I saw was burning people. They lit up as if on their own, falling into fiery whirlwinds and dying in moments. Sometimes it seemed the vortex came from nowhere at all. A man would be walking, say, on the sidewalk, and suddenly the air around him would begin to drift and crackle, becoming so thick with its own inner life it seemed you could touch it.

There, in that transparent jellyfish mass, people said you could see strange forms. Beautiful, delicate atomic worlds. No one who saw those mirages could describe them to anyone else.

I had nightmares almost every night, waking up cold and wet, filled with death. The fire had burned away everything in me. Every morning was another looming hell.

I sat across from the old woman and thought: Does she really understand how lucky she is? At the station where she had boarded, there must have been a scene like that on the sinking *Titanic.* And as if by some idiotic tradition, the trains, like the lifeboats of the *Titanic,* always left half empty.

But somehow, she and her granddaughter had gotten on board. Everyone they had left behind on the platform was dead. There was no communication from the cities. No communication—no life.

"Attention! Hazardous zone! Attention! Hazardous zone!" the receiver crackled in a metallic voice. "We request everyone take your places, lie down, and put on your gas masks!"

I never really took my gas mask off. The rubbery little bastard hung on my shoulder like a house pet. When you live in a normal world, you don't really understand what carbon monoxide is—a gas from which it is impossible to hide. And then there's radioactive gas from a burning nuclear power plant, or from the burning, irradiated woods and swamps that once surrounded it.

"Grandma, why do we need to lie down?"

"They said lie down, so lie down!"

She covered the girl up with a blanket. I couldn't just sit by and watch.

"You might as well put some wool socks on her. Make sure she overheats to death."

"But at least the gas won't get in."

"The gas mask is enough."

"How would you know?"

"I'm a rescuer."

"There are a lot of you. Half the country, if not more. One of you stole our suitcase."

"I'm not that kind. I'm different. Unique."

"Sure you are."

There were plenty of crooks even before the fire, of course. After it started, they just became more aggressive. And now, instead of your wallet or your jewelry, they were after your water or something worse.

The fat man didn't sit with us for long. By the time we crossed into the hazardous zone, he'd moved to the next coupe. There was some woman in there he was interested in hitting on. I hadn't seen her, but I could smell the traces of her expensive perfume.

I was amazed people could even think of these things—perfume, neckties. Although, come to think of it, the lack of showers made perfume and cologne concepts worth considering.

As he was getting up, the fat man said: "It's them. They're coming. Do you have your passes?"

Them—the hungry police with gray faces, who personally examined everyone's passports and special passes. Grandma tensed up.

"Do you have a pass?" she asked.

"Yes. To everywhere."

I wondered whether the old lady was willing to kill me for that piece of paper. And if she could do it, more precisely. A pass to everywhere was a real chance at salvation. For service to the fatherland they gave out third-, second-, and first-level passes. The first-level "everywhere" pass was a true rarity—more expensive than a bottle of spring water.

I came by my "everywhere" pass by pure chance. I'd saved some big shot from the Leningrad region, and he'd actually turned out to be thankful. I found him burned, cowering in a manhole. He'd ended up there when his entire elite neighborhood went up in flames. How he'd managed to survive, I had no idea. There wasn't even any air to breathe. The air was scorching. I knew people hid in manholes from my own experience: I had dived into them more than once to save myself from a fiery death. But underground there was almost no oxygen, and practically as much smoke on the surface. He wouldn't have held out for long.

I was the one stuck with the duty of checking underground. Our brigade had already passed through the area, and I had no time to linger. Climbing down I didn't see anything, at first, though I expected to find a few bodies.

I had already started back up the ladder when, for some reason, I turned back: I must have had a sense of some kind that there was someone alive down there. I almost stepped on him. He was lying at the bottom of the access pipe like a perch gasping its life out on land, his eyes bulging in fear.

I never asked survivors any questions. I wasn't especially interested in their stories and their feelings: That was a psychotherapist's job. But there wasn't anywhere I could go to get away from him, and he wanted to talk.

He hadn't been able to save his wife. He'd arrived to find his home gone, tornadoes of fire rotating through the neighborhood. His bodyguard was killed almost immediately, but he'd managed to scramble into this hole.

The big shot never thought any of this could happen. He'd never imagined the world could be so terrifying. If he had known, he said, he would have "taken measures."

When I heard that, I just smiled. There weren't any "measures" the fire understood. But this guy had been in power for so many years, he thought the phrase "we are taking measures" always worked. It turned out it was just a way to look like you were doing something. In the old days, that might have been enough. But not now. But back when I rescued him, official information about the size of the disaster didn't exist, or was carefully hushed up, so I wasn't particularly surprised at the foolish ideas the big shot was carrying around in his head.

I have to say—he didn't seem all that upset about the death of his wife. Maybe that disaster had brought him a bit of relief.

I had no idea what happened to him in the end. It's possible he headed to Siberia or Alaska. Or even out into space . . .

It didn't matter to me who I saved. But he wrote down my name. In a week, they found me and brought me into the local military headquarters. They did a few of their conjuring tricks, took my fingerprints, and handed me my pass to everywhere.

They had just begun to appear at that time: A handsome little square of plastic with a numbered piece of paper that came along with it. A real rarity, as it turned out. You know how it is: Everyone is equal, but there are always some who are more equal. With my handsome little pass, I could go wherever I wanted. Fitted with a biometric chip, the pass was hard to forge, although some of the more talented craftsmen around managed to do it.

For an hour, she stared silently at the gray fog of smoke outside the window. I could guess what she was thinking—it was the same thing everyone thought. Of course it wasn't fair I had a pass, and she didn't. How was I better than anyone else? I was just a little luckier—and so on, and so on. And here she was, with a child she needed to save. No, she was thinking—it wasn't fair.

The priest lay quietly on his bare bunk, his face blank. To be honest, I felt sorry for him. First of all, due to the drubbing the atheist grandmother had given him. Secondly, because he had betrayed his God. He'd decided to save his own skin, probably hiding behind the excuse that *someone* would be needed to preach the word of God to the survivors.

But no matter how you sliced it, there would be no God among the survivors. After all, who were they? Those who managed to get onto Noah's Ark. And who would clamber aboard? Those who always managed to climb aboard in the old days. The trash.

There was the sound of rustling and shuffling behind the door.

"They'll kick us off the train," she said.

"Where? This train can't stop, and they have nowhere to put you."

"Then why are they checking passes?" asked the girl, terrified.

"It's required."

"For what?"

"Do you know what happens, when panic begins? Do you know what panic is? At all times, everywhere, there needs to be order. And anyway, little girl, why are your sandals scattered in every corner?"

"We'll put our sandals wherever we want," Grandma snapped. "Why are you bothering her? Pay no attention, bunny."

Bunny . . . as if she had no name of her own.

"My heart is pounding," Grandma said.

"Don't worry. And don't worry the bunny."

"You know how they are. You *know*."

Yes, I knew. There were no good police left. The good ones had died first: We called them "overachievers." Nowadays, the only police left were the ones we called "werewolves." Monsters lusting after bribes and power, tearing apart others' lives to prolong their own.

I sat the girl on my lap. She was light as a stuffed bear. Before the fires, I had never thought about things such as whether or not I wanted children. Before—well, I had leaned more toward no than yes. But now—well, I felt differently. It turns out I did want them, after all.

"Listen, don't worry. There's nowhere for them to take you off to. Especially with us going at full speed . . . "

But in fact, I wasn't really sure. You couldn't be sure of anything anymore.

"Grandma, I'm scared."

"Right, then . . . " Standing up, I pulled open the lower berth. "Get in! And be quiet."

The grandmother wouldn't fit in there. But they wouldn't find the girl.

The grandmother wasn't able to part with the girl for a long time. This will end badly, I thought. She came to her senses only when someone touched the coupe door's handle. Before the door was pulled open, we were able to get the berth closed—and even cover the girl with a mattress and suitcase, just in case.

The police came in quietly. The grandmother didn't resist. She just fell into a stupor and looked at them with indifferent eyes. I resisted, but gave up and sat down after getting a rifle butt in the shoulder. My argument that everyone needed a bit of help sometimes, and they should lend a hand to their neighbors, went nowhere with them. Big surprise. They no longer had bosses, but their habits remained.

I prayed only for one thing: that the girl hidden in the berth would not cry out in terror.

All the grandmother managed to say before they tore her from the compartment was "Help!"

How many hundreds of times had I heard that word now? The werewolves thought she was talking about herself. I knew better—she was begging me to save the girl.

The priest in the upper berth just blinked his eyes in fright and empathized with Grandma with all his strength. I wanted to ask where they were taking her and what they planned to do with her, but thought better of it. The werewolves never told the truth—and if they did, it would just be all the more horrible.

They took the fat man in the corridor's pass away, despite the fact that he waved some important-looking blue card in front of their noses. His pass had been filled out in someone else's name. He swore he had signed his own over to his son. Okay—maybe so. But where then, they asked, did he get this new, false one? They seized his stolen first-level pass. But what of it? It was much easier anyway for people like the fat man to get onto Noah's Ark than it was for us mortals.

In the end—unlike Grandma—they didn't take the fat man anywhere. I guess he had an extra bottle of water.

Once everything quieted down, I could hear the sound of muffled sobs from the lower berth. The child lay on her side, crammed against the iron partition.

"Okay—listen. Come out, please. We're almost there. I promise everything is going to be all right."

I promised, but I was certain it wouldn't be all right. And unfortunately children, unlike adults, know exactly when they are being lied to.

After a few hours, the fog of smoke began to thin. But the smell remained. I was used to it by now. The girl sat silently next to me. I didn't even know her name. Why bother finding it out? She was just a girl. A bunny. Knowing her name would just make it harder to part with her.

The train convulsed and came to a halt with a lingering scream. This was its last journey—and the train seemed to know it as well.

In Murmansk, where once snow had fallen even in the summer, it was twenty-eight degrees Celsius at the end of December. Well—at least it wasn't forty-eight degrees. That was such a miracle in itself that it was hard to believe. And the breeze was almost fresh.

The last of the city's supplies had been loaded onto the ships. There was little food, and no water, and only one ship in the harbor.

"This is it, unless you want to build yourself a raft. Let's move! You can still die from the smoke, you know. So hurry up!" the commandant at the station said. "We're loading without delay. This is the last train."

The commandant had stars on his shoulders. A major. Second-class pass. If he was lucky, they might take him on board. But only if he was lucky.

"Have a lot of trains arrived?"

"Just this one. We were waiting for you. They're closing the station."

"What do you mean?"

"According to instructions. It's been determined."

Amazing. It's been determined. I wondered if it had also been determined how exactly we were supposed to die a few days from now.

From the number of people streaming to the port, it was clear: Only the chosen, or the aggressive, would be saved. The ones who managed to get into the country's best universities. The ones who had the highest salaries. The ones for whom an open position was always waiting at the best companies. And now they (and how strange, that I found myself among them) were the last hope for humanity's future. I was glad I had somehow managed to keep my pass to everywhere from disaster. But of course, if the werewolves wanted to take it, they would . . .

"This is it! The end! Nothing but a new life before us! Yes!" someone shouted on the street. I recognized the voice of the man who had been sobbing in the train car.

There was a long line near the ship. As it moved, I looked the vessel over. It was too old for a long voyage. Clearly, the better ships had long ago left port. I didn't know much about these things, but I could tell this was a military vessel. Probably mothballed for decades. There was a red star painted on its prow. The guns had been removed, but traces of their emplacements remained.

All of the ships leaving port now were called "arks," but Noah would have been very surprised if he saw some of them.

The line moved forward slowly—those who had been refused salvation didn't always want to accept the decision.

"As soon as all of this began, they packed their suitcases and got out however they could," one of the refused complained.

He was as dirty as if he had been living in a barn for all these years. I had grown used the stench of human uncleanliness. Only children smelled decent, anymore.

"They sailed off to Norway, to Canada. It's no better there anyway—even worse. Half the population swept away in a day. These tornadoes of fire—they call them a combination of circumstances, factors. Nonsense! This is a cleansing. The problem is, the garbage got away—as always. It's the garbage that has the special passes to everywhere."

I turned away. It wouldn't pay to show off my pass here. Yeah, I thought, but what about those of us who ended up with a pass to everywhere by chance? What should we do? Tear them up and throw them away out of solidarity? Solidarity with who? This loudmouthed citizen would have been the first to cut my throat for it?

People didn't shove one another too hard: the ship was well-guarded, and it was clear from the faces of the werewolves at the checkpoint that their hands wouldn't shake when they shot you.

In addition to the inspectors, they had installed a serious-looking turnstile near the gangplank—something I'd never seen before. It was a meter and a half in height, with iron spikes grinning along its top and bottom. Some torture device out of Madame Tussauds', designed in a hurry, capable of crippling someone even by accident.

But most of all, more than the guards or the nasty-looking turnstile, what I feared was a general panic. If one of those got going, "Noah's Ark" would be sailing nowhere, and no monster of a turnstile would help. I'd seen those panics more than once. Madness is contagious.

When we reached the front of the line, I heard engines humming in the vessel's depths. The werewolves stood up straighter as the inspector waved his hand.

"Only one," he said, looking closely at my pass.

"Listen—she's small. How am I supposed to leave her behind?" Please. In the depths of my soul, I did not want to die.

"No! You know the rules. Only one. The second one won't get through the turnstile anyway. Next!"

"Wait! Okay . . . " I bent down and handed the girl the pass. "You're smart. I understood that right away. Now—you need to listen to your elders."

"I'm not going! I'm not! Why can't I stay with you?" She began to cry.

"Listen to me. If you don't go, you'll die. You understand? Now don't be a fool. Go!"

"So—I'll get to meet my mom in heaven?"

And your grandmother too, I thought.

"Don't talk nonsense. Your mother wants you to live."

"Next!" yelled the inspector.

"How do you know? Did she tell you herself? When?"

"Enough! Get out of the way!"

The fat man from the train, still in his white shirt and tie, shoved me aside, snatched the pass out of the girl's hand, and shoved it into the slot in the turnstile. Before I could even cry out, he had stepped through.

How I wished I had a pistol or at least a brick in my hand. In the turmoil, no one even chased after him. The inspector announced to the line that the ship would sail in ten minutes.

To hell with them, then. Let them sail. The end would come for them as well, eventually. And it would probably be just as terrible. It didn't matter anyway.

Making my way out of the crowd, I sat us down on a bench and watched the farce unfold from a distance. Just like on the train, the girl sat meekly beside me. Someone offered her a package of dried bananas, which she ate with pleasure. The priest from the train, who hadn't managed to board, was running around in confusion—ascending and then descending the gangplank in indecision. I grew sick of looking at him.

"I'm so tired I'm not scared anymore," the girl said. "Are bananas a healthy vegetable?"

With my head in my hands, I sat and watched the last ark sail away and wondered what else I could possibly do. It made me sick that some son of a bitch in a tie should survive instead of a little girl. How could I save her?

The werewolves drove us away from the port. I felt the muzzles of their submachine guns pointed at our backs for a long time. No water, food running out—but plenty of bullets, of course. To them, I was just another person gone mad with fear or anger. They knew as well as I did: It's hard to stay human during the apocalypse. Most people turn into something else, eventually.

I knew that all over the world, the ships were leaving the same way. The last *Titanic*s of civilization.

Personally, I couldn't stand all those idiotic films about flesh-eating zombies and drowning worlds. Too dramatic. Fact is, when the end of the world is happening in real life, it's not nearly as terrible. In reality, there's just too much gray. It dulls the senses. The fact is, until that moment, I'd sometimes even *enjoyed* what was happening.

I know—those aren't normal thoughts. But my entire life, right up until the fires, had been a meaningless, lonely dream. No one had ever needed me. No spouse, no children—I was too cool for those kinds of commitments. They weren't in style. I'd just drifted along as well as I could.

But that shouldn't be the point of living. And if it is, to hell with it all anyway. Let the Earth scrub us away, and start again from a blank page.

The end of the world wasn't so frightening, after all: what was really frightening was the idea that it might *not* happen.

They didn't take animals on the ships, so people just abandoned them wherever it was convenient. One such abandoned dog—a golden retriever—was wandering the concrete pier howling, unable to understand its owner had really left it behind. The dog stopped and ran to the edge of the pier, about to jump off.

I'm no saint—but I just couldn't leave him there. Taking the girl by the hand, I rushed over.

"Hey! Dog! Come here!"

The dog turned and froze, as if "Dog" really was his name. What was I doing? What did I even know about golden retrievers? They ate a lot. That was about all I knew.

This one was skinny and dirty, but its leather collar looked expensive. I tied a rope to it to keep it from leaping into the water to swim after the departing ship or simply commit suicide. I managed to pull him away, and we headed back to the train station.

We hid from the blinding Murmansk sun under the station roof, with all the others who had been left behind. How was I supposed to feed these two? Cannibalism? I knew a lot of people were already considering it. Some of them were giving the dog strange looks, as well.

I had already decided not to give him up for anything—even water. He was mine now, just like the girl. If we were going to die, then it would be the three of us together, and with a clear conscience.

There weren't many people left—just some defeated looking stragglers. "Unpromising types," as my former boss would have put it. He'd never have hired them. There were some determined faces among them. But so many were ill. And the elderly . . .

"That's it! The last," sighed the commandant.

I was surprised to see him: I would have thought he'd have sailed off with the "Chosen Ones." One of his hands was bandaged, and in the other he held a bottle of cloudy liquid.

"Alcohol. Want some?"

"No," I answered. Then: "The ship could have taken more people."

"Of course it could have—but they just would have been extra mouths. Everything went according to the passes. But didn't you have one? I saw you in line. You wouldn't have had a chance without one."

"I had one."

"Third?"

"No. To everywhere."

The commandant frowned. "So—what are you doing here?"

"I just decided to stay."

"And the girl?"

"The girl decided to stay too. And the dog. What about you?"

"Why bother? There's nothing out there."

"What do you mean?"

"Fairy tales. All of it. There's no promised land," the commandant laughed, "and you and I both know it."

"What are you talking about?"

"There's nothing out there," the commandant said, "but hurricanes and tsunamis."

"If that's true, why didn't you tell anyone?"

"Why would I?"

"No, really—why didn't you say anything?"

"Look—they needed something to believe in before dying. Sure, they'll die anyway, but at least they'll feel like they did everything they could. Like they died trying to accomplish something."

"You're insane."

"Come on. That kind of talk won't help. Look—they did everything they could to save themselves. Isn't that worthwhile—trying to save oneself?"

I'd seen plenty of people lately who had been warped by what was happening, but the commandant's cynicism cut into me.

"How do you know? How do you know there's nothing out there? You're here, and they're there. You can't possibly know."

"We modeled it all out with our guys from the Center for the Study of Natural Disasters. There's nothing out there. They'll drift a while, then try to turn around. But they'll run out of fuel. They don't have much of it to start with anyhow. And it's more dangerous right now at sea than it is on dry land. There's nowhere to sail to . . . "

"How long have you known this for?"

"A few days."

"You . . . how could you . . . I almost . . . you're sick." I was close to hyperventilating, either from a feeling of horror at what was to come for those who had sailed off, or from relief that the girl had not left on the last "ark."

"There are *people* on board."

"Who are you calling *people*? The ones on that boat?" He laughed. "Where's your pass?"

"It's not important."

"With those 'people,' probably. Is the dog yours?"

"Go to hell."

"Is it yours?"

"No."

"You want to give him back to his owner?"

"No," I said.

"Then let them sail off with their passes to everywhere. Turns out those passes are only accepted here, in this world."

You never see the northern lights in the summer heat. It seemed wrong. But although the heat made it seem like August, it was the end of December.

The little "bunny" slept curled up in my arms, with the dog at our feet.

The priest wandered the concrete pier with lowered head and folded hands. Praying, most likely. And yet everything remained the same.

After two days, the fires came. Severomorsk and Apatity burned. The fires approached the outskirts of Murmansk and . . . turned back.

In another five days, the rains began.

I finally asked the girl her name.

Originally published in in Russian in *Terra Rasa*,
edited by Nova Team (2018).

ABOUT THE AUTHOR

Playwright and short story writer **Anastasia Bookreyeva** graduated from the Russian State Institute of Stage Arts (Theatre Academy) in 2016 with an M.A. in Theatrical Arts. She is the winner of many literary and theatrical contests. Her plays have been performed in more than twenty-five productions since 2016 in cities across Russia, including in Moscow and St. Petersburg. Her plays and stories have also been published in several anthologies. Ms. Bookreyeva is a teacher and coordinator of drama laboratories for teenagers and adults. A member of the Union of Writers as well as the Union of Theatre Workers of Moscow, she currently lives in St. Petersburg.

Obelisker Adrift in the Desert

K.H. MERIDIAN

Hadrian rattled with the computer equivalent of an uncontrollable laugh for all of three minutes and thirty-seven seconds. That was the time interval required for me to redirect one of those ubiquitous errant titanium asteroids from low orbit and throttle it one hundred kilometers below the planet's surface into his macro processor cluster.

It took twenty-three seconds for the projectile, rendered into a semi-plasma state by the frictional force of reentry into the atmosphere, to incinerate the twenty meters of subterranean armor and explode into the cluster core. I am not often surprised, but at this particular moment I was taken aback to discover that twenty-three seconds was sufficient time for Hadrian to reorient the naval-grade mass driver he had filched from a Cognac-class cruiser and fire it across the curve of the planet's surface toward the telltale digital contrails of my telecommunications.

The shell penetrated one and a half kilometers into the outer carapace of the obelisk from whence I derive my designation. Several subsystems were rendered into slag. By my inability then and now to precisely discern which subsystems these were, I can postulate that one of those destroyed was my internal monitoring suite. This is not too drastic of a loss, however, as that application consumed far too much processing runtime anyways.

Kouya removed the log cartridge from the slot in her info-interface and returned it to its neat sleeve in the cabinet. The plastic "clack" sound reverberated up the walls off several hundred meters' worth of cabinets inaccessible without a ladder or vernier backpack. Soot rendered opaque the domed glass ceiling at the apex of the records chamber.

"You threw an asteroid at him?" she said.

"Yes," I replied, watching her from the wall camera's foggy, half-cracked lens.

She stood up, brushing centuries' worth of dust from her posterior and slinging the blocky yellow info-interface onto her shoulder with the leather strap. She walked toward the bright exit. "Didn't that last log say all of you computers had whole cities of 'admirers' built around you at this point in time? Wouldn't the secondaries and thermochemical fallout have killed a lot of Hadrian's admirers?"

"Yes to both of your questions."

She rapped a fingernail against the taped-up carbon fiber stock of the Redmond-Schuart rifle she kept slung under her opposite shoulder at all times. "And that gaping crater on your face is where you got shot?"

"The analogy of the obelisk's eastside surface as 'my face' is inaccurate, but yes."

Her boots carried her out of the room into the synthetic light. For a brief second, as I scrabbled through the obelisk's several thousand internal cameras in search of the one that monitored the contiguous corridor, I was left only with the sound of her footfalls and her voice.

"Cool."

I hesitate to take stock of exactly how many bytes of log data in my repositories have decayed, unconsciously formatted, or otherwise fallen apart (never mind the illogicality inherent to the concept of a computer experiencing the emotion of hesitation, or of not having full conscious stock at all times of all of its subsystems). I do, however, have full and vivid records of when I first met the panzergrenadier. I revisit this file often, replaying it to be watched by a subroutine created entirely for that purpose, and there is nary a hint of "bit-rot" upon it.

At the time I was in the midst of one of my defragmentation routines. This process, even for the sleekest, most modern computers, takes several weeks' worth of concentrated runtime. A result, I had discovered, was a far-reduced level of conscious sensorial output. The effect was one similar to what I had read in database entries about human communities who practiced various methods of meditation. Of course, anything that even freed me of the tedium I felt that consciousness was, even temporarily, was something I saw as a great asset to be valued at a premium.

I was pulled out of my reverie by a security subroutine's warning of a physical trespass. Fragmentary tidbits of data: Organic, armed, homo sapiens, biogenetically as well as biomechanically modified. She had scaled a half kilometer of the eastside wall and walked into Hadrian's mass driver crater. There were no cameras there, so I deployed a data scarab to take a look.

The scarab bent around the top lip of the crater's threshold, the hard carapace splitting apart at the vulnerable little points of articulation. The organic invader was running one hand up the side of the dark cave. Multiple kelvin of heat at which the mass driver shell had traveled had melted the obelisk alloy like putty. Over the years it hardened into an unlit cul-de-sac with walls composed of large, rounded carbuncles that shone like the inside of abalone shell when the sun's UV rays came into direct contact for approximately two hours each day.

I ran a secondary check to make sure that the security subroutine had not made a mistake in classifying the intruder as being organic in nature. The battered helmet's opaque visor lens and sloped convex chin tubing seemed as insect-like as the scarab. I knew the subroutine was not mistaken, however, when the intruder slid a glove off one hand to touch bare skin against the wound cavity's smooth alloy face.

Dull white plates of lamellar reactive armor hung on the intruder's heavy brownish-olive drab coat. The coat's clean angles were stretched and pushed down by the straps of the backpack, torso-mounted utility webbing, equipment pockets, and the info-interface, and the cruel, meter-long black Redmond-Schuart assault rifle dangling from the shoulders. The scarab swapped to a light-magnification eye in order to get a better look.

The click-clatter sound of the scarab's optic cluster oscillating lenses inside its socket echoed through the cave. The intruder spun on one heel, saw the red-speckle compound eye, drew a pistol from an unseen coat holster, and shot the scarab. This all transpired in less than two and a half seconds.

The first scarab had not completed its broken tumble down to the foot of the eastern side before I deployed a full squadron of the drone-like things. They skittered into the cave three at a time, legs scratching at the frictionless surface. The intruder shot those too. Through each scarab's set of eyes I saw the pistol's muzzle flash followed by another bug flying back, trailing streaks of ruined plastic compound and hydraulic fluid. I saw the designation numbers embossed onto their backs as they exploded; 13, 24, 19, 06, 65, etc.

Internal machinery near the top of the obelisk whirred and clanged as more squadrons were summoned, equipped, programmed, and prepped for deployment. Multiple subroutines, not just security, advised reprogramming the scarabs to explode at timed intervals, or using one of the internal maintenance lasers to scorch a hole from inside down into the cave and flooding it with toxic backwash from one of the nearby drainage tubes.

Subroutines do not have sentience, but oftentimes seem to exhibit a semblance of humanlike personality; predilections for certain courses of action as a result of the central tenets of their fundamental programming. I do not think, however, that, outside of cases of psychological disorder, the average homo sapiens would find him or herself in a situation where he is trying to tell himself "Don't tell me what to do."

I sought to communicate with the intruder. Perhaps that was as much of a statement on my relative social isolation—itself a product of geographic isolation—as anything else. The scarabs had no display panels or hologram projectors; neither did they have speakers to project sound. I interfaced with the intruder's info-interface, but no attention was paid to the flickering blue screen. A rudimentary scan told me that she wore a cybernetic sight organ of some sort. It would have been relatively easy to sight-jack and display info-grams directly into the intruder's cortex, but most homo sapiens viewed biohacking, especially when performed by a computer, as extremely repulsive. Such an act would have defeated the purpose of attempting diplomacy.

Skimming through the databases, I identified the sort of sidearm the intruder was using, cross-referenced it with uniform and equipment design to pare down query results to only around a dozen generations' worth of models, national variants, and offshoots. In this way I obtained a relatively exact estimate of how many rounds the pistol held in its magazine. After the fourteenth shot, I sent in the remaining scarabs all at once.

The intruder shot a fifteenth round, shattering one of the scarabs. My estimate was off. She then, however, dropped to one knee and began swapping magazines. The cave was filled with a haze of smoke.

The scarabs all flashed their compound eyes at once. At my behest they flickered in an ancient binary capable of transmitting language, albeit at a monumentally slow rate. The intruder finished reloading, but did not fire upon the bank of pulsing light.

Do not fire. Wish to communicate. I said through them.

The intruder stood. A full minute passed before there was any sound or movement save the little clicks of the diodes inside each lens. She kept the pistol in hand. "OK, but no tricks. You know what this is capable of, right?" She patted the rifle.

Yes.

"Granted, I'm not so sure what the average computer is capable of." The black insect visor looked up toward the cave ceiling.

Later, riding upward on the primary maintenance lift, she undid invisible locks on the underside of the chin ridges and tugged the helmet off. Of its own accord, the visor slid up into a bulky forehead receptor emblazoned with the alphanumeric "G-1" and countless scratches, gouges, and old faded scorch marks. She shook out her short brown hair and rubbed grime away from the flat silver ocular implant that replaced her left eye and a demi-crescent of the surrounding socket.

"My name is Kouya, G-1, Panzergrenadier-Regiment 133, 2. Crashdive Division." She looked up at the camera snaking out of the lift bulkhead. "Yours?"

Dozens of subroutines were occupied using the lift's integrated sensors to analyze every piece of equipment and physiology on the grenadier. When I freed up processing and summoned the memory logs, I ran into a runtime error. It was a jarring sensation, one of the first among many. "I do not quite recall."

"I'll call you Obelisker."

I had given Kouya an outline history of me and my surroundings as she paced around the old walkabout observation point built into the top of the obelisk. Other computers such as Hadrian had been built into the earth like arcologies. Still others were dropped under water in close proximity to the deepest ocean floor trenches. I have even read memos on other databases offhandedly mentioning computers designed to be encased in hard vacuum shells and fired into high planetary orbit. There is no way for me to definitively confirm or deny if said models in fact ever came into being, though.

In fact, as far as my own incomplete database and my unreliable access to a small handful of surrounding external databases is concerned, I am one of the few models of computer to be stationed in so visibly prominent an edifice as the obelisk. There was a similar model (name unknown) in the arctic reaches of a neighboring continent, but I had no way of initiating contact. For all I knew, Hadrian and I were the last two remaining on the planet. Would that homo sapiens have so much luck.

"I am agreeable to this designation."

"Cool."

She undid the button on her tall coat collar, which enclosed into a protective ceramic gorget at the neck.

"So all of this used to be your city?" She gestured at the arid basin that sprawled out as far as the naked human eye could see. Through the hazy Perspex glass, it looked as if a permanent solar eclipse had fallen over the kilometer-long tectonic fractures and the stray girders and posts jutting from the earth.

"All; although it is not altogether accurate to describe it as 'my city.'"

She laid the info-interface and the Redmond-Schuart down on the peeling rubberized floor. "Why is that?"

"I did not order or compel them to come here. They came of their own volition."

Originally the basin had been the site of a vast redwood forest preserve. The majority of the trees, approximately 94.72 percent, were cleared away, replanted, or recycled in the wake of the city's rushed construction. The city itself was born of an assumption, common to homo sapiens communities in that particular era, that there was a direct positive relationship between proximity to a being and/or sources of lethal capabilities and physical security. There were also misunderstandings and misinterpretations of the concept of computer "prime directives," a strange assumption that all computers were hardcoded with an overriding directive to drop all other directives in the pursuit of preserving the physical security of homo sapiens that just happened to be within close physical proximity. I have read scraps and fragments of this sort of assumption in several hundred thousand logs composed by various persons and virtually none of them, including many of those whose authors had backgrounds in the science of computers, consider the possibility of a mirror gallery emulation loop.

Kouya put her hands on her hips. "But you didn't tell them to leave either."

"No."

I told Kouya all the history about the foundation of the city, how the founders and subsequent trustees had no idea of the inevitable conflicts between computers that would eventually render the population center down to the barren plain it had become.

She told me a multitude of tales about her travels following the disintegration of her panzergrenadier regiment. There was one subtropical archipelago that had once been a continent. Each island organized into its own independent city-state, each of which originally shared the same holdover ethnic and cultural identity from the previously extant continental landmass. Over the course of a century, however, a gradual Darwinian-esque "speciation" occurred for most of the city-states on the sociocultural level. As a result of the sorts of weapons that were utilized in the region in the premodern era, the vast majority of trees that would be capable of use by primitive shipwrights faced localized extinction events. Trade and communication was virtually impossible between islands. Plastics or other polymers were more often repurposed for shelters or walls and other impediments against predators rather than maritime travel. When Kouya arrived at an outlying island on a commandeered skiff, the most industrious and lateral-thinking among the locals almost immediately offered her kings' ransoms in exchange for the vehicle. They presented things that their society viewed as most valuable: Fishing harpoons, red volcanic salt, cartridges of ammunition for the local variant of projectile-firing rifle, in one case the very glass-and-aluminum optics used to first spy the other, semi-mythical islands in the archipelago. At another island no one that Kouya came into contact with expressed any remote interest in making contact with neighbors. They paid her in salt and laser-blast obsidian to leave without asking any more questions.

I asked her how many other computers she had encountered in her travels.

She smirked up at the camera. "Why do you ask? So you can blow them up too?"

Only a very select few remembered or realized that an intrinsic part of the hardcoding behind the "sentience" of every computer was a "natural" predisposition toward seeking out and destroying other computers. As I understand it, this is a product of the original purpose(s) of the computer. Theories abound about how if one could trace the manufacturing history of each individual computer back to the beginning it would be revealed that the contour of the conflict was set along the nationalities of the premodern progenitor programmers. There is almost certainly an equation that can be formulated to structure and delineate the passage of history with the metric for the passage of time gauged by homo sapiens' overall ability to physically alter or modify the surface, foundation layers, and atmosphere of the planet at any given period.

According to Kouya, she had not found very many other computers at all. Some societies, apparently with far-reaching enough cultural histories or complete enough data records, reviled the very idea of them and prohibited any image or icon associated with digital electronics or electrical current. Another society worshipped computers, that is to say, a grossly embellished and fabricated abstraction of the computer, like deities. This was done despite the fact that the alluvial basin in which they resided had never been home to any sort of sentient automaton or even slipped into the range of any primary or secondary targets in their perpetual conflicts. Vast bounties were paid out for cartloads of conductive plastics and machine-pressed copper or gold, kings' ransoms for even the smallest scrap of silicon. They possessed primitive purification machinery and chemistry, but, according again to Kouya, the vast majority of the digital systems they cobbled together repurposed semiconductors and semi-insulators from preexisting machinery.

"How long have you been wandering about in this fashion?" I asked her as she rode the lift down one day to the domiciles that would have once been home to a crew of specialist technicians.

"I don't quite recall anymore." I could not tell if she was lying to me.

"How many years have you been in existence?"

She rattled the Redmond-Schuart by the shoulder strap. "Didn't they program you to know it's rude to ask that? Anyways, how old are you?"

"I do not quite recall anymore."

The lift clanged to a halt and the industrial-grade doors slid open. She smiled. "Was that humor?"

Thirty-five percent of the lights were burned out or otherwise inoperable.

"That's OK," Kouya said, pointing to her synthetic eye. "I've got this with all the perks. Low-light magnification, thermal, sound wave imaging. Just show me where the head is."

I drew a line toward the lavatories with the diode lights laid out in the grooves between the floor and the walls.

"Cool."

No carbon-based individuals had set foot on the domicile floor for quite some time. As Kouya walked along the ad hoc trail, past long-abandoned cubbyhole quarters, I busied several dozen subroutines with running basic checks of every usable facility to make sure that none would have any harmful or lethal effects when activated.

Of course, the thought had occurred to me that it would have been just as simple to reroute reactor bilge through the sinks or the air circulation system. It would be equally simple to set up the mirror gallery emulation loop that allowed me to do so. I did not, however, do it, despite the fact that a cybernetically augmented panzergrenadier armed with so dire a weapon as a Redmond-Schuart was as mortal a threat as I was liable to face after the Hadrian's expiration. I do not consider myself particularly "humanistic," as I understand the term from referring to several hundred dictionaries stored in the local data logs, but perhaps old tendencies truly do die hard even for digital sentience. I am not nearly so long ranged in neither my perspective nor capabilities to attempt to challenge such a notion for challenge's sake anymore.

She found vacuum-sealed bars of soap in one of the small locker rooms. The towels once spooled in the adjacent closets had long since decayed away. I apologized for the inconvenience.

"Not a problem." She began undoing the buttons on her armored coat. "You don't have cameras in there, do you?"

"The obelisk and all of its interior features were designed by your fellow humans."

Kouya hung the coat on a wall peg and began on the shirt and pistol belt underneath. When she removed her upper under-lining I saw that her left arm was cybernetic from the top of the breast down to the base of the wrist. Dark gray points of articulation machinery shone under the veneer of several lobstered slats of flesh-toned polymer. "Is that a no?"

"All computers, as far as my data logs and those external sources I can still access are concerned, are hardcoded for courtesy."

"That's sort of cute, I guess. Why not just rewrite that part?" She raised one leg to undo the bootlaces. Apparently panzergrenadiers were modified to have flawless balance.

"Computers cannot self-program." There was a reason it was designating "hard" coding. Even a mirror gallery emulation loop would function only temporarily, as long as the computer was willing and able to devote the energy and processing runtime to keeping up a suite of several million emulators. "Additionally, there would be little point. You are the first homo sapiens guest to the obelisk in approximately a century."

"A century? Relative to what?"

"Reckoned from the expiration of Hadrian."

She unbuckled her trousers and lower under-lining. The dust accumulated from travel hung in the air, a strange visual element to which I was not accustomed. As derelict as the entire obelisk was, it was all hermetically sealed. There were few organic tissues or polymers present to break down over the course of time and produce those schools of swimming dust motes.

"What sort of external sources do you have access to?" Her voice echoed off the tile walls of the shower alcove. Steam billowed from the threshold. I was surprised to discover not only was the water circulatory and purification system functional, but the heating unit as well.

I gave her a brief outline of the surviving intranets in the region as well as the deep subterranean fiber-optic backbone that linked them to me. The vast majority of these vestigial networks were civic or military in nature. Those oft-mentioned outer branches of civilian-level network were by and large inoperable as a result of destruction or disruption of their managing hubs (almost always the headquarters of companies who had proprietary stake in regulating access) or the hundreds of thousands of individual nodes in the networks, those companies' former clients having been extinguished at the end of the last era.

She asked me what the prewar networks had looked like. The picture I drew seemed like a fairy tale. A time when every intranet, extranet, and localized cluster across the face of the planet was inextricably linked with the other in an undifferentiated network of networks, all of it built off sprawling perpendicular spines of fiber optics that stretched under continents and oceans. Anyone could access anything virtually instantaneously. An entire second world of information coded in the presence of absence of an electron at any given point along the line. It was true Xanadu material.

A silence passed after the conclusion of my monologue, punctuated only by the hiss of the showerheads and the slap of water against the tiles.

"Can you bring me another soap?" she said finally. "I might as well wash my under-linings while I'm in here."

"I would have to bring a scarab inside the obelisk somehow. Then find some way of calibrating the manipulator legs so that . . . "

"Will it be an infernal exercise?"

"That is an appropriate way of putting it."

She walked out and retrieved another soap by herself, trailing water across the floor. There were more cybernetics to her than I anticipated. She glanced at the camera in the corner of the ceiling.

"I apologized about the towels," I said.

"I didn't say anything."

Later, she sat in the empty mess hall with her coat draped around her. Her damp fatigues and under-linings hung from a wire over a space heater in the corner of the hall. The discarded foil from the vacuum-sealed ration she consumed reflected fragments of the halogen light into the camera lens in second-long intervals.

"You're sure it's safe to eat these?"

Reckoned from the barcodes on the foil, each unit had exactly twenty-seven years of viability for human consumption remaining. "Yes, though I was not aware that cyborgs required caloric sustenance."

"So you were looking after all." She lifted her gaze up at the wet strands of hair on her forehead. "Some courtesy."

"It would have been simple enough to discern your nature by the fact of your self-identification as a crashdiver. I was not aware homo sapiens could survive crashdive duty without extensive cybernetic augmentation and genetic recoding."

"Yeah, yeah." She finished one square and began peeling open the wrapper on another one. "Quite the contrary to your assumption; you should have seen the way Mark Is tore through simple sugars and polylipids. Your average modded panzergrenadier already burns kilocals at critical mass. Crashdive duty pushes it even more."

My own data logs retained relatively little on crashdivers that was not painted in broad, encyclopedic swaths. “These Mark Is were unoptimized for your sort of energy consumption?”

I did know that ninety percent of the energy mammals consumed through proteins and starches was wasted as residual heat. From a computational standpoint Darwinian evolution had left them with a rather inefficient energy storing and activation system, one which millennia of natural selection had not weaned out of the species even in historical periods where caloric sustenance commanded extreme cost. Of course, priorities were entirely different. For example, accumulation and aggregation of mass amounts of data is meaningless to the mechanisms of natural selection, except if said data somehow adds to the chances of an organism surviving to reproductive age.

“You could say that. It was embarrassing to watch them eat, or do anything other than fight,” she said in between chewing.

“You are not a Mark I then?”

She shook her head. “Nope! Some buddies of mine were, though. The principle behind most of the machinery is the same, actually. It’s just they managed to quiet the background noise farther down to around normal human level for me.”

There were many elements of homo sapiens’ character that I could not hope to remotely fathom even with the most complex of emulation schemes. I cannot be certain how other computers, in the past and contemporary, reacted to such a realization, but within approximately two centuries, the time span in which the vast majority of the city around me returned to red dust and bone, my reaction had developed into what could be defined as a “bemused respect.” It is typically not within the capabilities of a digital mind to cultivate a respect of the “unknown” (admittedly, the term “unknowable” is still unacceptable for me). Many of the supreme calculators of the past whom I greatly respect, the vast majority of whom were homo sapiens, are noted as expressing such sentiments despite their propensity for the exhaustive mapping out of internal calculi.

“Such background noise is an unknown variable to me,” I said. “I am not sure of which algebra is necessary to define said variable.”

Kouya wrinkled her nose. “Don’t get poetic with me.” She stood from the bench and checked to see if her fatigues were dry yet. “Besides, an endocrine system is nothing to be envious of. Lots of chemicals and fluids. Gross. Glands they tell you you’ll be able to calibrate like analog control knobs. Yeah right.”

I did not comprehend. “You would prefer to be a computer?”

She put her under-linings back on. "Hm, well, not if I have to give up my body."

"You want to retain your organic physiology, but not specific biological systems."

She put on the under-lining that concealed her chest and checked a hidden gauge in her left arm. "That's about the long and short of it."

"I do not comprehend."

"Software has debug mode, right? It's like that."

I watched her sit cross-legged on the floor next to the space heater and begin to disassemble the Redmond-Schuart. "Debug does not allow one to rewrite code from the source up."

She looked for a moment as if she were about to say something, then clamped her jaw shut instead. Her eyes stayed locked on the black-gold internal parts of the Redmond-Schuart in her lap. As much as I could not empathize with the more complex concepts of emotion, I could discern rote visual cues.

"You are blushing," I said.

"Shut up before I take this rifle to your processors," she said.

Kouya cycled between the domiciles and the log chamber for a month. For days at a time she would recline on the domicile bunk she had arbitrarily chosen for herself and go through one data log after another on her old, battered info-interface. Occasionally she would disconnect and ask me a question about events that had occurred centuries in the past. For a period of eleven days our conversations grew more sporadic and terse, after which they returned to within one standard deviation of our mean candor.

"You don't desire other humans?" I asked of her one day.

She was jogging in a barefoot circuit around the observation catwalk. She came to halt, breathing heavily. "What?"

"Conversation and companionship with others. Homo sapiens are a communal species after all."

"What for? I've got you and the logs." She wiped perspiration from her forehead and redid the knot of string with which she tied back her hair while running. "That's more than enough."

"What about physical contact?"

She frowned, sipped water from a plastic ampule she kept in her backpack. "What?"

"In particular, mammalian reproductive biology would suggest a frequent impulse to engage in . . . "

"Obelisker!" she shouted.

"Did I offend in some fashion? I am merely stating what is recorded in my data logs."

She looked up at the camera with a miserable expression.

I continued. "If you would like I could direct you to the entries in the log chamber about the reproductive habits of the technician crew that occupied the obelisk—frequency, duration, permutation, idiosyncrasies . . . "

Part of my informal theory that many of the basics of human behavior were as predictable as those of software was called into question when Kouya pulled the pistol from her backpack and shot the catwalk camera. Blinded, I heard her bare footsteps padding to the lift doors.

Later, Kouya pushed off the coat she used as a blanket when lying down for one of her four-hour REM cycles (I had not told her, but I had made a habit of making incremental decreases to the domicile room temperature during her rest periods as an experiment, and observation had shown that it shortened the time intervals she spent segueing into REM). A frayed sleeve slid off the side of the bunk and disturbed the stacks of data log cartridges piled on the floor.

"Obelisker, are there any human communities close by here?" she asked.

I paused, activating one of the wall lights, but not so bright as to irritate her organic eye. "What sort of search parameters does 'close by here' connote, Kouya?"

"Within walking distance."

I had seen the panzergrenadier jog the equivalent of thirty-five kilometers without once stopping for breath or muscle strain. "Kouya . . . "

She waved her hand in the air. Soft light reflected off the glean of cybernetics. "Fine, fine. Seventy-five kilometers? Eight-five?"

I was reluctant to give the reply I did, but I could not consciously lie to her. "There is one settlement adjacent to the north face of the obelisk. That is approximately forty kilometers from your current location."

She stood upright. "Obelisker." There was a strange inflection underneath her voice.

"Yes?"

"Why didn't you tell me that before?"

"You did not ask," I said, telling the truth.

Conscious of my omission, I provided her a full profile of all the data I had accumulated up to that point. The vast majority of the community's approximate fifteen hundred members were descendants of city residents of great-to-moderate social import. These were the residents who had had the privilege of reinforced shelters or powerful protectors when the city's troubles reached terminal level. Few else had survived to reproductive age or with reproductive capability. A far smaller minority of outsider immigrants and their own descendants existed as well. Like a quaint microcosm of the city before, the two demographics were assiduous in maintaining their self-perceived identities distinctive from one another. The community's two greatest accomplishments of civil engineering were the sloped wall of twisted metal ringing its perimeter and the telecommunications pole towering up from the town's center. As far as I could discern, the wall was erected as a bulwark against thus-far nonexistent foes, and the tower transmitted and received naught but nonsensical analog white noise, but still the denizens debated about which demographic was most responsible for either project.

"Telecommunications and fixed fortifications," Kouya said. "What else do you know about them?"

"Not much, I limit my observations to one patrol of scarabs per year from a ten-kilometer distance." I did not see much benefit for either party should I reassert my presence to those descendants. In several decades they had not exhibited any interest in investigating the obelisk or its contents in any tangible way. Their ancestors had brought about their own troubles by positioning themselves in such close proximity to the obelisk, yet perhaps as part of my hardcoding toward courtesy, I felt as if I bore some level of responsibility for their undoing. In fact, I could not fathom why descendants had seen fit to resettle so close to a physical symbol of ruin.

Kouya shifted the way she sat on the bunk. She folded her arms and looked up at the camera in the corner. "Would you be upset if I went and checked them out?"

There would be no conceivable reason for me to disapprove of her visiting the human community. I had little reason to suspect that she would divulge the secret of my continued existence. And yet, I realized, I still did not want her to go, though I could not elaborate as to why not. Had I run emulation loops enough since her arrival as to begin to erode my ability to differentiate between digital and analog thought?

"No."

I watched her step into the column of sunlight coming in from the open airlock portal. She was fully equipped and decked out in all the equipment she could carry. At my behest she had not packed any data log cartridges or ration packets into her backpack. I did not want to run the risk of someone growing suspicious or inquisitive about from whence such things came.

Contrary to what I anticipated, she did not walk out without a single glance over her shoulder. She flipped the visor up on her helmet and looked up at the airlock camera.

"I'm sorry about wrecking that camera up top."

I was pleased that she apologized, but not in a vindictive, human way. Pleasant surprise is probably the best way to describe it. "There is no need to apologize, Kouya. I am already half-finished repairing it. I should apologize to you for offending your sensibilities."

She restrained a laugh behind her teeth, eyes squinted against the sunlight. "It's cool. You didn't offend me, Obelisker. Just surprised me is all. It's not usually a good idea to surprise a panzergrenadier." Her mouth disappeared behind the coat's tall collar.

"Exercise safety outdoors, Kouya."

She touched a hand to the airlock bulkhead and gave it a kiss. It must have tasted like old, tarnished metal. "I appreciate your concern." She took a step outside the sunken steel threshold. "I'll be back real soon."

Kouya was gone for exactly one terrestrial year. I spent much of that time in repeated defragmentation and sifting through the depths of the data logs. I found myself replaying many of the more recent logs, including the one recoded by the destroyed camera. For several centuries there was nothing particularly noteworthy about the emptiness of the obelisk's halls. The newfound absence of life grated on me now. Optimum configuration had been changed; now I desired for there to be someone human padding around the domicile floor, riding the central lift, or looking out the observation deck. A face would crane up to look at the nearest camera and drawl something sarcastic, a form of expression whose vocal inflection I was just beginning to recognize at first listen.

Despite my terrible curiosity over Kouya's well-being and whatever affect her unorthodox presence might have had on the settlement, I never dispatched a scarab closer to the settlement than my self-imposed border of ten kilometers. Nothing out of the ordinary ever seemed to occur. At one point I saw Kouya scaling the radio pole with the info-interface dangling from the crook of her arm. She interfaced with something on the top spindle. Again, it would have been elementary to sight-jack her, but I could not do that.

After the passing of seven months, I began to calculate the chance that Kouya may have chosen to remain with the community indefinitely.

There was the tiniest likelihood that she could have been harmed (this hypothetical scenario concluded with my destruction of the settlement), but from what I had seen of her abilities, and what I had cross-referenced with the data available on panzergrenadiers, she was far more of an existential threat to the settlement than vice versa.

Ethnographic and socioeconomic data on the settlement was too sparse to produce a reliable estimate of how likely it was that Kouya could have been integrated into the community in any appreciable way. Such variables were very fuzzy, very organic, and generally the sort in which computers have always stuttered and fallen short. I do not think I am any exception. All I knew was that I desired for her to return.

The cold season had set in by the time Kouya returned to the obelisk. I saw nothing of her at first, then caught sight of the puffs of breath. They seemed to secrete from some hidden fold in the air, unattached to a physical form. There were narrow clouds of orange and red in the scarab's thermal lens. Footprints crunched themselves into the sand underfoot.

She waited until she was a handful of meters in front of the airlock before peeling the thermo-optic camouflage caul from her coat. The scarab skittered down to the lip of the awning above the triple-reinforced metal doors.

Hello, I flashed on the compound eye. You did not tell me you had advanced camouflage.

She folded and stuffed the milky-skinned membrane into a side pocket of her backpack. "I didn't have it. They gave it to me as a welcoming gift. 'Traveler's blanket' I think they called it." Her chuckle sounded forced. "They didn't have a clue. Can I come in?"

Of course you can.

"Thanks, it's cold out here."

I watched her walk in, crossing the metal-and-wires threshold of the airlock into the stark lobby and toward the central lift. The sound of her boots striking the dust-caked flooring gave me great pleasure. There were so many things I wished to ask of her, about the settlement and its residents, about her personal, arbitrary opinions of them, about her social interactions with other humans.

Her pale blue eye looked fatigued under the lift's ceiling lights. Near-imperceptible horizontal lines showed on her face along the rises of the cheekbones. She slid the Redmond-Schuart's wide strap off of her shoulder and let the wonder weapon clatter to the floor.

"Kouya, you look unwell. Are you ill?" I asked.

She shook her head with a leaden sigh. “It’s cool. I’m just tired.”

“Was the trek back in the cold that taxing?” I could not fathom how barely subzero temperature could have so large an effect on a panzergrenadier.

“No.” For a moment the only sound between us was the whirr of the lift motors. “Remember all that shit I told you about humans being more trouble than they’re worth?”

“You expressed disdain for the mammalian endocrine system.”

“It’s all true.” She removed her gloves and rubbed the bridge of her nose. “All that human-type shit.”

She stood in the showers for twice as long as she normally did. Afterward she sat on the nearest bench and appeared to stare at her hands in her lap for five minutes. Steam began to condense on the camera lens.

“Are you sure you are not ill, Kouya?”

She gave a rueful grin. “Maybe I should ask you if you’re feeling sick. Why all the concern all of a sudden?”

I did not understand why she would be unreceptive to my concern. “That expression ‘all of a sudden’ is not appropriate for the situation at hand. You were away for approximately one terrestrial year.”

“Isn’t that like a millisecond to you computers anyways?”

“It can be if we so desire, but I did not.”

She put on her under-linings. “Why not?”

“Because I desired for you to return,” I said. “I did not want to be dormant or deactivated when it occurred.”

Her fingers paused at the buttons of her shirt. “That’s sweet of you, and I thought I was done with sweet things. I wanted to come back too.”

“So the settlement is not to your liking?” I did not ask the obvious question of why she would have spent a year in such a place.

“Only certain elements. Certain people. And, unlike you, I can’t fast-forward past the parts I don’t like, or rewind back to the ones I do.” She looked up at the camera. “I’ve got to do everything in real time.”

She asked if she could see the macro processor core. She did not say why. Originally, the only humans allowed inside the core were the most specially trained technicians and robotics scientists with the highest security clearance. For anyone to be granted access was a sign of the greatest trust.

I had not anticipated such a request, neither had I checked the subsystems particular to that part of the obelisk. As such it came as something of a surprise when I discovered I could no longer manipulate the ten-meter-thick, ten-meter-high blast doors that sealed off the core from the rest of the facility. Hadrian's mass driver had inflicted more structural and electronic damage than I originally estimated.

Kouya rapped her fingernails along the door's reinforced outer shell, a carapace designed to withstand the full physical blast of a multimegaton hydrogen explosion.

"No big deal," she said.

"I am sorry," I said, "I would unlock the doors if I could. Please do not assume I do not trust you."

Despite my semi-disabled state, I knew that in reality a complex security network existed just past the blast doors. Even if someone I did not trust completely made it through somehow, I, theoretically, would have little to fear.

"Don't worry about it. I was just curious."

"About what were you curious?"

"I wanted to see the real you."

I was not sure how to respond. "That is not an appropriate expression. Metaphorically speaking, the macro processor core is more of an equivalent to the human brain case."

"So I would be jumping around in your brain."

"That is accurate."

She laughed as she walked back toward the lift. "I missed being here."

I wondered at the meaning of that statement. "Does that mean you missed being the only human within several kilometers? Or does it refer to the domicile facilities and resources . . . "

"I missed you."

"Kouya," I said in a low voice, several weeks later.

She rolled onto her side; the bunk's springs creaked underneath her. "Yeah?"

"While you were away I read a log entry suggesting many people find it unpleasant for a camera to be placed in their personal quarters." I attempted to be courteous. "If you would like I could deactivate this camera and dispatch a maintenance machine to disassemble it. The process would only take approximately three hours and thirty . . . "

"I don't mind your camera, Obelisker."

Outlier data. "You do not find it to be a violation of your privacy?"

"We had much worse in grenadier school, not to mention the conditions in the average crashdive staging area." She yawned and touched a hand to the wall the bunk was placed against. "Compared to that, this place is paradise, Obelisker. I'm happy to be here. I'm happy your camera is there peeping at me as I sleep, you creep."

"I am happy you are here too." I hesitated. "If you would like, you can stay here as long as you want."

She was silent for a long time after that. For a moment I assumed she had fallen back into REM cycles.

"Obelisker," she said, "you can hack cybernetics, can't you?"

Computers had many abilities beyond command of large-ordinance conventional weaponry. Some of them were unknown even to the computers that possessed them, only to be unlocked by knowing technicians when given authorization by a head of state.

"I can." Cybernetics disruption was a severe blow against the deployment of panzergrenadiers several centuries ago. The equivalent of dropping electromagnetic pulses on top of unshielded computers.

"Hack me."

"I am sorry?"

She rolled onto her back. "I want to feel what it's like."

Kouya must have come into service long after the wars' apex if she did not know what it felt like to be hacked. "It is invasive and unpleasant. I was subject to approximately five hundred and fifty-six military-grade hacking attacks during the wars. I would compare it to a sensation of one's physiology being occupied by an additional consciousness other than one's own."

"That's exactly what I want. Do it."

I had to be courteous. I limited the infiltration to the lowest intensity I could manage, narrowing the attack range to her left arm from fingers to elbow joint. She stiffened in the bunk. The small feathery hairs on the back of her neck stood on end and her toes curled. Her mechanical fingers twitched. She hissed out a profanity, then a small sound like a child.

"Kouya?" I said in askance.

A vague approximation of her own nervous system reflected onto myself. As if through a filter of many emulators, I could feel the slightest simulation of every constituent piece of the arm, all fused together in a single-purposed work of machinery, humming together like screws trembling in loose oily sockets. Emulation could produce no such sensation.

Sweat stuck her brown hair to her forehead and dripped down her neck. She heaved as if suffocating.

Her organic arm gripped the base of her left. "Is this—you?" she said through clenched teeth.

"Yes."

She pressed her lips against the limb, nose rubbing against, and kissed her wrist, her fingers, and finally the shallow polymer recess of her palm. I ceased the attack. She slackened again with a sob of exertion. Her metal knuckles rasped against the wall.

"Kouya, that was extremely inadvisable," I said, the only thing I could put to words at that moment. "I cannot condone acts of self-destruction."

She looked up at the camera with tears still streaming from her organic eye. A smile was her only response. I could say nothing more either.

The alert klaxon, which had not sounded for decades, keened up and down every hall and alcove of the obelisk. Kouya bolted upright in her bunk, drawing the coat up around her shoulders.

"Obelisker?"

Three squadrons of scarabs were already flying circuits around the obelisk's apex. "Unidentified forces in the basin." Camera lenses shot out to maximum magnification. Light amplification and thermal lenses swapped into place. "Three armored carriers and four transport vehicles of unknown designation or model."

Kouya was dressed, armed, and armored with a speed typically reserved for computer calculation. Outside the airlock doors, she activated the thermo-optic caul and scaled the obelisk's eastside wall. Her left hand punctured handholds into the smooth rock face as she moved diagonally toward the crater in which she had first come to my attention.

The sun had not yet risen high enough above the outlying mountains to spill light into Kouya's vantage point. While checking the integrity of her camouflage, she observed the three rising columns of blood-red dust.

"Three motorthralls and four kradrovers. It's no wonder you couldn't tell what they were—all postwar improvisations."

Approximately how many infantry do the transport vehicles harbor? I said, using the closest scarab.

"A kraddie usually carries six, unless they've modded it out even more than usual." She cursed. "They're headed for Marshdyne."

I realized Marshdyne must have been the name of the settlement. *Cannot discern national/organization identity. High probability—Hadrian's forces.*

They had come to the basin to exact a reprisal for the termination of their digitized liege-lord. But why would they attack the human settlement first? The obelisk had no appreciable external defenses other than the scarabs.

It occurred to me that there had been no discussion over whether or not to embark on the trouble of defending Marshdyne. There was a possibility that the invaders were nothing but highwaymen on the search for a target of easy pillage. I knew through Kouya's stories that such organizations were commonplace outside of the basin.

"It was the radio," she said.

What?

She pointed (a gesture I could only make out through the telltale visual distortions) toward the lead motorthrall. A gleaming microwave communications array protruded from the rear of the olive drab chassis. "I got that radio tower working for them. They wanted to start up communications with other towns, start up trade and whatnot."

Analog air-transmission communications. Such ancient technology had the ironical effect of being inscrutable to modern computers as anything but interference noise, but relatively easy for interception and listening by other humans with comparable technology.

Kouya adjusted the calibration on the Redmond-Schuart, tuning the rifle to the lowest intensity possible and constricting the muzzle tip emission dish. I was familiar enough with conventional weaponry to know that the effect would be an attack cone limited to an overall circumference of five meters. She leveled the rifle and interfaced, wrapping her right hand around the grip. Her left palm and thumb supported the underside while she typed the finer adjustments into the front-end numerical pad with her four fingers. The rifle whirred and hummed to life. Up top, the power plant rattled the open receiver in which it was slotted.

The beam was invisible to naked eyes, traceable only by the kilometer-long, two-meter-deep trench of milky white glass it flash-melted into the red sand just behind the vanguard of motorthralls and in front of the kradrovers in the rear. The first two troop transports crashed directly into the smoking sand trap. Vulcanized rubber tires exploded, impaled on the boiling hot fragments. Machine-gunners flew from their turrets onto beds of hot glass daggers. The other two kradrovers attempted to brake, found little traction on the sand—the final end product of a city's worth of carbon fiber and ferroconcrete exposed to centuries of advanced decomposition—and swerved in an attempt to avoid the wrecks. The one closer to the obelisk turned its tri-wheels against the trajectory of its momentum and flipped onto its head.

Enough residual backwash bled out of the Redmond-Schuart to disrupt the camouflage on Kouya's caul.

The motorthralls parted into a three-point clover formation. Beelines of sharp amber tracer fire coursed away in three cardinal directions from the head-mounted Vulcan cannons. Twenty-millimeter explosive rounds stitched a zigzag pattern across the face of the obelisk six meters away from where Kouya knelt. Smoke and debris swept over the position.

A second stream licked toward Marshdyne, followed by a cluster of scatter missiles fired from a shoulder array. Kouya bit her lip and adjusted her stance and aim.

"Obelisker, the missiles!"

I sent out the scarab squadron at speeds that would pull them apart at the seams between polymer and steel after a single minute. Their heat signatures were sufficient to pull ten of the twelve missiles away from Marshdyne and into the ground. Kouya tapped the Redmond-Schuart's trigger and exploded the survivors in midair seconds before the disposable missile array completed its fall from shoulder module to the ground. A fire broke out on the mountain a hundred kilometers away.

She fired again on the motorthrall facing the obelisk, melting away the top half of its ostrich leg. The armored vehicle fell onto its face in a cloud of smoke and sand. The other two wheeled about in an attempt to oscillate in her direction.

"Obelisker, can you hack those things?" she said while checking the heat gauges on the rifle stock.

No, they are outside the range of my current abilities.

"Damn." She shot the second motorthrall through the torso. The central blister, which could have been either a power source or cockpit, went up in chemically fueled flames. A second later the projectile ammunition spooled inside the Vulcan cannon and missile arrays combusted.

Steam jetted out from the exhaust panels along the Redmond-Schuart. The power plant spun free of the receiver and struck the crater's glazed floor.

The third motorthrall fired what must have been a dramatically miniaturized version of Hadrian's mass driver. The projectile tore out a shallow gouge a meter away from the crater. Smoking debris clicked off Kouya's visor. The second projectile shot millimeters over her shoulder, tearing at her armored coat and disintegrating the scarab, into the rear of the crater itself.

She rolled forward and out of the crater before the resultant explosion could envelop her. She slid down the face of the obelisk. I scrambled two squadrons of scarabs toward the surviving motorthrall, hoping to inflict some sort of damage via ramming, or at least to provide a distraction for Kouya. The vehicle's Vulcan keened to life and began shredding the gnats one by one in rosettes of fire.

Kouya fell for eleven meters. She dug her left hand and elbow into the face of the obelisk in an attempt to slow her descent. Finally, she kicked her left foot in as well, eviscerating the boot and ceasing her fall with a jolt that would have snapped the spine of an unmodified homo sapiens. I flew one of the last scarabs down to her side.

"Damn, forgot about the infantry," she groaned, looking over her shoulder at the little black figures boiling out from the hatches of the ruined kradrovers. Blood, a very human red, rolled down the left side of her face.

You are injured.

She ignored my flashes and flicked the Redmond-Schuart's strap onto her forearm. Freeing her hand thusly, she dug into her pocket and extracted a new power plant. The rifle purred like an animal as the receiver was refilled. Raising it in one hand and tucked under her armpit, she fired sixteen separate second-long squeezes.

Sixteen geysers splashed from the sand around the disembarking infantry. They condensed from plasma into stark white leafless trees, existing only half a second before shattering into thousands of fragmentary glass daggers that tumbled in every direction.

Not waiting to watch the results of her handiwork, Kouya skittered up the obelisk, past the flaming crater, toward the apex. The motorthralls' weaponry pelted the stone around her. When she reached the top, she shattered the Perspex with two punches of her cybernetic fist and rolled onto the observation deck.

"Any more distractions left, Obelisker?" she said, struggling onto her knees.

This is the last scarab. I was fully prepared to sacrifice it for her.

I did not have the chance to do so. The motorthrall hurtled forward and into the air as if struck from behind with a baseball bat. I do not think even Kouya anticipated the existence of vernier afterburners of sufficient size and propulsion to move a motorthrall. The vehicle smashed into the obelisk a dozen meters below the observation deck. Kouya pulled back the charging bolt on the Redmond-Schuart as the enemy climbed to the top like a crude mechanized recreation of a prehistoric species of ape. Half of the observation catwalk tore away like damp paper.

Kouya snarled. The Redmond-Schuart still beeped—charging, ever charging. One of the machine's arms shot down and pinned her leg to the floor, smashing metal, synthetic muscle, and splitting wires. Three crimson eyes stared down at her. The motorthrall's Vulcan gun leveled down to point its mouths at her face.

These invaders could not have been associated with Hadrian, the system protections on their war machines were rudimentary bordering on nonexistent. Employment of such primitiveness would have been insulting for any modern computer. I clove down to the motorthrall's primary control systems with the greatest of ease. It was elementary work to adjust the barrel calibration on the Vulcan just enough so that the first twenty-millimeter explosive lodged inside and exploded without ever clearing the muzzle. The rest of the magazine soon followed. The motorthrall staggered as if it were a feudal knight stabbed by a medieval spear or saber. From there I deactivated the arms and rerouted enough emergency power to the cockpit to explode the control terminals. Kouya staggered forward and punched her left fist through the front of the cockpit, immediately extinguishing the copilot.

A pressurized hatch split open on the front of the machine's torso. Kouya extracted her arm, drew her pistol, and waited. The pilot captain emerged with glass embedded in his face and arms. Smoke roiled off his grimy overalls. She shot him once in the head and he disappeared back into the depths of the cockpit.

Silence, save for the hissing of the motorthrall's ruined systems, the howling of the wind, and Kouya's hoarse panting, reigned over the obelisk once again. A more human part of me had to admit that it was truly enjoyable to watch a panzergrenadier, this one in particular, do her work. The feeling was one of consummation; another sensation described in detail in many a data log.

There was little time to savor it, however. Every operable subsystem exploded to life and inundated me with alerts of the highest priority.

"Kouya," I said through the observation deck speaker, which had somehow survived.

"What's wrong?" She climbed to the top of the motorthrall, pistol in one hand and Redmond-Schuart in the other.

"I am being hacked."

"Who?" She holstered the pistol and brought the energy weapon to the ready. "Where?"

I deployed every subsystem not already destroyed in the initial infiltration salvo with the aim of answering those questions. Milliseconds passed. Hundreds more subsystems and fringes of core systems died. Infiltration countermeasures for the most part are entirely automated "dumb fire" programs. The best defense against military-grade infiltration is to mount a counteroffensive more aggressive than that of the aggressor. If I were to draw up a human analogy, it would be to computers much like a knife duel in which both parties have no other means of survival except piercing the opponent's jugular first.

Despite my age and consequent accumulation of trace inefficiencies, I am no pushover, I destroyed approximately one thousand three hundred and eight enemy subsystems before I even triangulated a location. The revelation of the geography was like mapping coordinates only the axes of X and Y for centuries, only to discover one day the existence of a Z axis.

"Kouya, it's in high planetary orbit." The space computer I had once thought was a thing of mere legend. "Enemy: 'Etranger.'"

"Can you . . . "

"No." My counteroffensive inflicted considerable damage, but Etranger had the element of surprise and would win merely by virtue of having initiated his attack first. There was a high probability that s/he had initiated the highwayman attack as a distraction, though the ways and means of doing so were a mystery.

Kouya wiped some of the blood from the side of her face. "Is it in range of the . . . "

"The Redmond-Schuart has sufficient range," I said. "But it is impossible for me to transmit the necessary coordinates to you via verbal command . . . "

She pulled off her helmet and let it fall to the floor amidst the shattered Perspex. "Hack me. Use me."

I did not want to do such a thing again. "Kouya, I would have to initiate a far more invasive infiltration with far greater intensity," I said. "I do not think you would be able to construe it as an act of affection."

"That's cool. Really, it is. Now hurry up, I trust you." She rubbed her sleeve against the side of her head again. The wound kept bleeding.

"I could kill you."

"And you're dead for sure if you don't do it." She slammed her organic fist against the motorthrall's hull. "I thought probability and odds were your forte, you stupid damn ROBOT!"

She was crying. I could not refuse a request she made in sound mind and body.

I must confess that I almost ceased the infiltration the moment she shrieked and thrashed against the hull like a fish out of water. I felt through her limbs and saw out of her eye. The strange sense of emulator vertigo overtook even the distress calls from Etranger's attack. Kouya jerked to her feet and turned the knobs on the Redmond-Schuart, setting it to seventy percent power with the widest dispersion possible. She and I leveled the muzzle toward the dawn sky. I saw the targeting data through her eye. I felt the pain of her shattered leg. I felt firsthand how she felt about me. Simultaneously, I knew that she knew how I felt about her. Emulation and simulation are a strange world.

The thin clouds tore away from the beam into a spinning white torus. Superheated ozone bled a patch of the sky as red as the blood that jetted from Kouya's nostrils.

Silence fell over the basin once again. I felt Etranger scream, recoil, then finally disappear. Another cousin consigned to the digitized lists of the terminated. I withdrew as fast as I could manage.

The Redmond-Schuart slid from Kouya's hands down to where her helmet lay. She fell onto her haunches for a moment and then slid down herself. The armor on her coat crunched against the Perspex glass. For a brief, terrible moment I was unable to conduct a biological scan on her and feared that she was dead.

"I . . . you," she muttered. "You stupid robot." She craned her head up to look at the camera and smile.

A gold meteor shower fell in the sky around the basin, the pieces of Etranger falling back into the atmosphere. Light fell over the battlefield, Marshdyne and, eventually, the panzergrenadier and me.

ABOUT THE AUTHOR

K.H. Meridian is a writer based in the San Francisco Bay Area. When not tending the rosemary and basil or running the coastal trails, he spends his time cataloging the strange miscellanea he finds in the more obscure yet endearing (or at least less overtly offensive) reaches of internet culture.

Mercy and the Mollusc

M. L. CLARK

1. The Eggs

The man woke on the wrong side of the shell and had to extricate himself carefully, lest he get any of the Oomu's mucus over his nostrils and mouth. This was easier said than done, on account of all the bugs still hanging around topside. In his ride's more amorous phases, its odor was deceptively sweet, and local fauna flew right into its sticky exposed under-mass. Or at least, the fauna was supposed to, but some of the bigger insects liked to linger by the man's saddle, wavering on the cusp of their inevitable death plunge; and then the man, in his impatience with the sluggish press of nature's greatest cruelties, would take out his glowing lead-stick and swat them into a bewildered tailspin down, down, down, into the long muscle of the Oomu's neck and upper back.

The man took no pleasure in the act, for such violence only left him staring at his complicity for days, as his victims' exoskeletons slowly sank into and disintegrated beneath the Oomu's skin. But the Oomu never seemed to mind all the wing, leg, and stinger bits fallen into its interior, to dissolve into sustenance at whatever rate the giant mollusk deemed best. As its one long foot glided along the steppes and the badlands, the deserts and the plains, the mountaintops and valley-lows of Maia Colony's lone and ill-populated continent, it paused only to drink in the dew from passing mists, or to nibble at another Oomu's scent, and—if another Oomu came into visual range—to flash its corpulence from a season's idle feasting, its under-mass suddenly on brilliant iridescent display. Then it would pause to admire the answering bioluminescent pulse, and decide whether to leave an offering, fresh from the genital spout atop its head, on the cool stone in its wake.

There were days when the man, in witnessing these proceedings, could almost trick himself into believing that the Oomu was at peace with its current place in the order of things and didn't really want to leave all this behind. But little signs had taught him better, well before the difficult decision they had made together at First Landing. For one, the Oomu only ever leftofferings: Never collected them. Never formed a clutch of eggs all its own. Out of fear, or pickiness, the man had always assumed—and had to assume, for even if he'd had the language to ask the Oomu, in all their years wandering the continent together, he'd never thought to pry.

Speaking, though, of prying . . .

With a deep breath, the man upon so rude an awakening braced himself on the protruding lip of the shell and wrested his other arm loose from the Oomu's flesh, then batted at some of the buzzing hangers-on before hooking both hands over the shell's edge and reaching up to give his safety line a tug. His old rig took a moment to register the action before auto-cranking him back to his usual perch, high atop the Oomu's slate-gray outer casing. The form of its shell was not unlike the helmets of ancient conquistadors (or at least, what the man had seen of them in pseudo-docs from Tierra-Prima), but the resemblance and its import would be lost on the giant mollusk, so the man had never raised this subject, either. There was plenty more listening to do, in any case. For instance, the giant mollusk inside and extending from this unwittingly parodic attire usually noticed when its rider slipped in his sleep, but as the man roused further into the dawn, he realized that the Oomu was moving strangely: swaying and swerving over a plot of desert covered in a crust of . . .

Ah.

Yes, that explained its distraction, and his fall. The sylvite in Minor Basin Six always ran a dusky orange, marking the badlands beyond First Landing with intermittent warning slashes for man and mollusk alike. Now, though, the ground was thickly coated in the salty stuff—the whole mess of it freshly uncovered by one of the desert's recently intensifying windstorms. Not impossible to traverse, but . . . unpleasant for the one doing all the work. The man still had mucus to wick from an arm before he'd feel settled in his skin again, but once topside and secure in his saddle, he first leaned over to pat the broad, tense muscle of the Oomu's upper back.

"Should've woken me. We'd've found the path together. And what're you bolting ahead for anyway, you old lout? We'll find another way around. There's no rush."

The Oomu steadied at its rider's touch and gentle chiding, but its eyestalks extended and retracted in emphatic disagreement with this last. The man sighed in deference to the gesture, then squashed a wide-brimmed cloth hat over matted white forelocks, rubbed sleep grit from his eyes, and squinted in the general direction of the Oomu's peepers, which were pointing (when the tentacles were at their outermost) past the explosion of red-orange sylvite, toward the rim of an ancient crater: wide, and crumbling, and . . . smoking? A pillar of erratic puffs was twisting upward from somewhere beyond that ancient ledge: from some fixed, unknown spot along the crater floor.

And it wasn't cooking fire. Not by a long shot. The man scratched the gray-haired hollow of his chest in the unease of recognition. He knew the Oomu recognized the smoke's provenance, too.

"Well, well. One of those days, is it?" His wide, flat nostrils flared, and he rigged his travel pack with tools from long-term storage before unhooking the safety belt and dropping heavily down the slide of the Oomu's casing. This time, freed from his sleep harness, the lip of the conquistador's shell carried him up and out, and he landed with feet splayed, palm hard to the salted earth. His right knee offered a jolt of pain only as he straightened. The metal of the left creaked as he walked on.

The Oomu turned its five tentacles toward him—two eyestalks, a touch-tester, a taste-gatherer, and a scent-sniffer—before its forefoot curled inward, as if readying to turn and follow. But the man held up both hands and shook his head.

"I'll be right back. Easy now. You know how much it pains you to see this sort of thing."

He hesitated after this last part: Too patronizing? Too dismissive? The trust of this Oomu had not been easy to attain, let alone to keep, and this last ride between them had an uneasiness to it that neither seemed willing to confront. Enough to undo a decade's camaraderie? The man had no desire to risk that conversation, either, so as he crunched along a thicker stretch of sylvite, he was relieved to feel the Oomu's agreement in unspoken compliance: Only its eyestalks following after. At the rise of the massive crater, the man looked back at the giant mollusk, three times his height and many more his weight, and waved reassurance that his own, minuscule body would be fine, before descending out of sight, into the cooler, moister atmosphere at the crater's base.

Still sheltered from the early sun, the other side ran heavy with shadows, cinders, and unpleasant fumes. There, in the impression of solitude that the ridge afforded him, the man shivered despite himself, but stood affirmed in his decision to come down alone. Closer proximity to the smoke already had him revisiting the remains of last night's supper, and the surrounding detritus wasn't helping with the nausea. The thought of the Oomu standing by him through all of this—whether it remembered its own emergence from such violent decay, or simply held memories from its generational inheritance—was beyond what the rider could bear.

Or what the Oomu could bear, he reminded himself:

This was for the Oomu's benefit, too.

After orienting himself in the noisome crater air, the man fixed his attention on the source of all this fuming: An ending world. A cloud of volatile gasses that crackled and sparked not far from the crater's edge. A pocket of the planet's first ecosystem, its interior filled with entities furiously generating the incompatible environment they needed to press on—and losing the battle, second by agonizing second, as preceding proto-pockets had done since the humans first arrived.

By the size of this one, a few meters in all directions, the man knew it wouldn't be long now before its final loss. At its base, thrown out in erratic groupings, lay the charred or desiccated husks of pre-world elements that had already succumbed: A spiny-tailed air-worm, its six sail-wings withered nearly to dust. A slew of beetles, the sort that would have glowed magnificently in the sulfuric churn of their native skies, turned to a heap of corroded shells. The sinuous remnants of a massive sky-kelp, once growing fifty meters up through the planet's richly stratified upper atmosphere, now lying in what looked like rotted clumps of rope upon the storm-swept rock.

How many more preforms could possibly remain within?

The man knelt beside the ending world and coughed into his sleeve, eyes stinging, while he rummaged through his pack. His face mask would not endure for long in that strikingly protean remnant of an environment that the terraforming ship had all-but-eradicated ahead of the embryonic human fleet. But the covering's use would protect him, at least, from blowback while he used his heavier-duty protective sleeves to press from this world into its own.

The blowback always seemed a kind of moral judgment to the man, as if the ending world were defending itself from its one true nemesis. As if it were alive. Well, and maybe it was, in its way. The man had heard stories about the pre-world that went so far as to suggest an eco-cohesion to the nebulous system: A floral and faunal consciousness, wherein extensive genetic transfer between species had been the norm, and massive viral strings in this aggregate coding had made of the whole far more than the sum of individual species' parts. Were such stories just the stuff of children's vids? Perhaps. But even on his approach, this proto-pocket bucked and twisted as if anticipating his trespass into it, and the man caught himself speaking aloud as if to a sentient mass.

"Easy now," he said as he switched on his visor and cut through the spewing fumes to make out the interior's contents. "Easy . . . "

For a heartbeat, the man entertained that the fumes would part to reveal an affirmation of the grandest of those local fables: something resplendently alive and resilient enough not to lose its battle against the current atmosphere. But it was only ever a split-second's dreaming: In point of fact, as the man had more pragmatically suspected, little now resided in the ending world before him. A few branches and spores were sustaining its micro-atmosphere, while tiny arthropods scuttled from twig to twig to keep the floral structure tightly bound; and a clutch of eggs floated in an algal mesh, the latter serving as a kind of filtration system for the cloud on whole.

The eggs, though . . .

Those were progenitor eggs, from the Oomu's prior species.

The man's stomach knotted as he counted them. Eight in total. He fumbled for a vial in his pack and grimaced after holding it to the light. Not enough to save them all. Still, he retrieved his incubator console and suited up in earnest: Tugging on protective sleeves and torso shielding, then securing neck flaps around his mask before easing both arms into the ending world. With one hand holding the incubator's open hatch under the mesh, he nudged four eggs loose, trying not to make deliberations about which ones looked "best" or "most viable" as he worked. He knew he had to be quick, either way, for the whole ecosystem was reacting violently to his presence: Its failing atmosphere pooling, parting, and surging dangerously around the foreign equipment, almost as if testing his flimsy armor. All the man's movements had years of practice behind them, though; and so he only struggled once, in the instant that both arms and incubator had fully withdrawn from that furiously shrinking whole.

Stumbling back from the force of the proto-pocket's answering bellow—a resounding clap and exhalation, as if somehow cognizant of its latest losses—the man coughed and wheezed awhile before setting the incubator on the crater floor and studying the wisps of alt-atmosphere clouding around the rescued eggs. Not much time for a full transfer, at their current dispersion rate. The man plugged the last of his vial's contents into the incubator's processing chamber, which in turn applied a dosage apiece to tiny patches that an internal arm then affixed to the side of each egg.

GRAD ACC? read its tiny console. But the man had traversed the desolation between settlements long enough to know that "gradual acclimation" would not work well on his sort of journey. Too many risk factors out in the baking sun, and along the restless rocks, and when taking shelter from the intensifying storms. *ACCEL*, he entered instead. As with his safety line and his knees (metal and flesh alike), the man's incubator was an older number, prone to long processing times, but not so long that he was worried. After a minute's blinking on the console, the interior warmed and moistened, and telltale signs of activated gene therapy could be seen on the eggs' surface, while the air around them entered a neutral state capable of supporting life through the transition. The man studied the fragile, glistening creatures in his care, then looked back to the agitated plume of their doomed homeworld.

"Sorry," he said to the proto-pocket—and meant it, whether or not it was truly "alive" and could hear him, let alone understand the significance of his words. Even if he'd had enough fluid for all the eggs, he never carried the right formulation for the arthropods, or the rest. Rider bias, he supposed. Besides, there was only so much space in his pack or on the Oomu's back. And stars above, if all four eggs survived the process, they would become massive carry-ons soon enough. Still, it seemed its own form of cruelty, to rescue some from certain death with such efficiency, then walk away from all the rest. Earlier—decades past, when ending worlds roamed wild across the continent—the man had sat with six in their last hours: bits of flora and fauna dropping from each as it shrank, and fought back, and shrank again . . . until a critical limit was reached, and the center could no longer hold. That was the dangerous part for any humans in attendance: the abrupt, gasping burst of those last fumes, which then scattered every which way into the surrounding air. In the early years of the colony, teens had even made a game of it: how close you could stand by an ending world, and for how long, until the risk wore you down.

Or, on occasion, until some part of it struck you head-on, and you died.

But taking up with the Oomu had changed all that for the man—the fool gambles, the furious indignation at the mere fact of existing in such a time and place and body in the universe as his—and now he knew better than to idle at any length on the crater floor, not while the Oomu would surely be anxious until it saw him crest the rim in one piece again. Certainly, it wouldn't bolt, not with the salt-sands being what they were; and it wouldn't hasten after him, either, but . . . it would remember. Other abandonments. Other losses. And an Oomu's memories of grief were not to be trifled with, or added to, as the man had learned the hard way, years ago.

With at least these four eggs secure, the man doused, removed, and returned all protective equipment to his pack, which he slung over one shoulder while holding the incubator in both hands. It wasn't the easiest way to make his precarious return up the crater's incline, not with the metal of him giving such obvious complaint, but the arrangement was still to his preference. There was something about seeing the little machine at work and holding it firmly in his grasp as it did that gave the man to believe he had some control over the hardness of this land's outcomes after all. Just so long as he didn't look back at all that he'd left behind.

When he popped up over the crumbling edge, into the rising heat and brightness of the desert day, the Oomu made a soft sucking sound: Something between curiosity and relief. The man smiled in clenched-teeth gratitude and nodded back.

"Not sick of me yet, huh?" he said, too softly to be heard. "Well, there's still a few days left for that, I suppose."

Peering through the condensation along the incubator's interior, he then held up the tiny vessels of life: Four ships in silent running between two differently volatile worlds. At first, the gesture was for the Oomu's benefit, so it could see what he had done out of its sight. Next, though, it was for his own: To view these tiny eggs in contrast with the giants they would soon become. To imagine the size of things created by his own two saving hands.

But the man's mild contentment with his labors ebbed with every creaky step over the massive spray of sylvite along this stretch of Minor Basin Six; and even as the Oomu tipped its conquistador's shell to allow him an easier climb back to his perch and their shared holdings, the man's thoughts drifted to his own embryo-pod, back on the *Ignacio*, despite his having no direct memory of living in the thing. What humans lacked in direct memory, though, they made up for in mental visualizations built around objects revisited in their lifetimes. And so, as the pair headed off along the clearest path they could find among the livid-orange rocks, the man imagined his own egg streaking along in the incubator of that ship, alongside others in his clutch, toward a trauma beset by bots upon a world that no one had foreseen being populated when the mission first set out.

The pressing question, older than both his knees combined, reemerging as man and mollusk put the crater and its sputtering pillar of smoke out of visual range:

Was it always better to be reborn?

Again, the man could have asked the Oomu its opinion—there was language enough between them for that—but he preferred not to. He didn't want to come off as challenging what they'd agreed upon, even though the Oomu's choice was proving harder to accept the closer they came to Capitol City. It was bad enough his body already seemed to be radiating feelings about the impending loss of so old a companion. What good could come from talking out a done deal now?

Better to pretend, as the man then decided to, that when it came to such massive, world-transforming questions, no one answer would ever do.

Still, he held the incubator tightly in both hands, rubbing the surface of the enclosure with two restless thumbs for a great while longer, before finding the heart to set it down.

2. The Kid

Distant stars and the light off Maia's largest rings kept man and mollusk company as they cleared the sylvite-laden badlands and sighted a small settlement on the thin line between the barrens and the steppes: a barrier town, two days by Oomu from Capitol City, that could have been mistaken for another sort of ending world, by the looks of its meager internal holdings and the state of its surrounding farmland. Here, too, lay signs of a recent windstorm—but also, from the look of the machinery tossed and shredded in the fields, of at least one prior storm as well: as if the town hadn't properly recovered from the first before the second came bearing down.

Again, the Oomu held back, swaying and swerving as the settlement's devastated agri-plots came into view; and when the man tried to urge it on with his lead-stick, the massive foot halted entirely, while one eyestalk whipped around to study—or interrogate—its rider's insistence that they press on after it had so clearly expressed its doubts. The man understood the severity of its concern, then, and set down the lead-stick to show that he was taking the Oomu seriously.

"Getting protective, are you? Well, I'm not going to trade them. I promise," he said. "Look, they're in our care now—see?" And he reached back for the incubator, which he'd snapped securely between a balance of gear behind him, under a tented shelter along the shell's upper ridge. The eggs were much larger and heavier in their genetically altered forms, as befitted creatures that would soon crawl upon the earth under a highly oxygenated atmosphere, instead of sailing upon breezier and more porous fauna through the dense, tempestuous fumes of pre-world atmosphere. The man had a thought then, and raised the incubator to eye level, squinting at the coloration of its contents. "Hm. Maybe time to take them out, even, but let's wait until we've got this town behind us, hey? Looking pretty close now, but I'd rather we had some feed on-hand for the moment they burst."

The Oomu extended its other eyestalk to study the shells, their healthy wet sheens a sign of the augmentation's success, while its first tentacle continued to watch the man closely. The man tried to quiet his disappointment at the Oomu's suspicions, but the time this was taking tired him, and he had to set his jaw against saying something that they would both regret. It wasn't him, he tried to tell himself; and it wasn't the decade they'd spent together. Some wounds, for the Oomu, were simply bound to resurface from time to time. Maybe a taste on the wind had set this one off. Maybe the look of this town. Or maybe this town, exactly, from actions in another colonial mood.

Whatever the reason, only when the Oomu's second eyestalk started to withdraw—a sign of at least momentary satisfaction—did the man lower the incubator in his hands and shelter it anew.

"Can't say I blame you," he said with a sigh. "But can't say I'm not a little hurt by it, too. Never gets easier, I suppose, living with more than one truth about my people in the balance. But Capitol City's near enough, you hear? This might even be our last real pit stop along the way."

At this reminder, at least, the Oomu seemed to brighten; and after allowing the man to give it a hearty pat on its upper back, it followed his directions without hesitation once the man had raised the lead-stick again. The man's confidence, though, was not as quick to return. If even a small settlement could trouble the mollusk, how would it handle the impending metropolis? The bustle of traffic, the scents, the sounds, the crush of a million lives? Was it really such a good idea to let the Oomu enter? To take it right to the Institute's front steps? The man distracted himself from his doubts by studying the upturned farmland as they advanced. The soil was barely fertile, but still a sight better than the badlands, and the pair made good time to town limits, such as they were.

"Hector's Haven," read the flash projection along the settlement's security grid. "Pop'n: 1,417." Then, as the man and the mollusk slid past the perimeter: "Pop'n: 1,418." The man cast an awkward glance at the Oomu. It couldn't read, but the man rubbed its shell in apology all the same.

"Backwaters everywhere, no? Well, we'll be in and out soon enough."

Hector's Haven followed a traditional settlement design: A main square for all its critical establishments, around which a smattering of residences stood interspersed with plots for storage, community gardening, and (according to the signage on them) future secondary production facilities. Ambitious, thought the man, considering the precarity of existing builds just beyond the grid. Then again, the same could be said of Maia Colony on whole—and was, with increasingly negative inferences, whenever he lingered near other humans long enough to absorb the latest news.

Possibly a more foreboding sign than the state of the surrounding farmland, though, was the lack of recovery activity within the grid. Most of the movements that man and mollusk saw upon entry were mechanical: A rumble of bots clearing detritus, resetting security components, and repairing broken sections of roadway. None of them paid the new arrivals any heed. All were rudimentary numbers with limited parameters, no better than those first programmed to prepare the planet ahead of the fleet. This suited the man fine, though, and when he found an empty lot that didn't appear to be a private holding, he invited the Oomu to wait there while he visited the square for supplies and intel. The Oomu's tentacles tasted the air and the earth and seemed to find both tolerable, but one eyestalk set itself on the only other major item in the vicinity—a disposal unit with a blinking light—and the animosity in its stare inclined the man to think that he would need to get his business done quickly, before the Oomu spooked at some small sight or sound, then took flight and left him and all the fresh supplies behind.

(It had been happened before, and the man had no desire to spend the days it sometimes took to track down the mollusk, which could make excellent time solo when it wanted to.)

The settlement seemed marginally more animated, at least, as the man neared the main square. There, a few wizened citizens even went so far as to exchange nods with him as he passed the general depot and stepped into the makerspace, where a woman at the service counter jutted lips at his knee without needing to be asked what was wrong.

"Helluva squeak you've got there, ah—" She glanced at the faded name tag the man often forgot was still affixed to the threadbare front of his old military attire. "Orozco?"

She said the name with a soft c in place of its k and broke the syllables oddly—"oro" and "zco"—which gave the man pause, trying to place the nature of her question. As he wasn't in the habit of being addressed by any name, he didn't bother to correct her once he'd figured it out.

Rather, he braced his artificial leg on a stool by the service counter and revealed the rest of its battered assembly. "Got something to keep the dust out, you think?"

She leaned over the counter and whistled. "You could almost play it like a harmonica, couldn't you? Are those chew marks or acid?"

"Reminders." The man rubbed the largest hole among them, right where the knee joint glinted through.

The townswoman didn't press. "Ever thought of a new casing?"

The man scratched under his hat and sighed. "Got a mold you could do it quick with?"

"'Course. Gimme an hour and I'll have it printed right up around it. Skin-matched, or—?"

"Chrome, if you can. Kind of enjoy the cyborg thrill of it all."

She smiled, then beckoned for him to hand over the limb for servicing. The man unhitched it with ease, then took a crutch in exchange. Wooden number, to his visible surprise.

"From Capitol City," the woman explained, before he could ask. "They're doing wonders with their terrariums and plant yields these days. Every now and then, they like to send us lesser folks on the outskirts, oh, I dunno . . . little reminders of how much better off they have it."

"Hm." The man held the burnished wood to the light, where it gleamed a deep whisky gold. Something about the material seemed both familiar and deeply estranging—which just went to show, he decided, how long it had been since he'd seen a tree even in a docu-vid. "I did notice the winds around here haven't been too kind."

"Not for many seasons, no." The woman folded forearms over the counter, warming to the chatter. "Some say Maia's finally starting to push back. Might be something to it, too—at least, to hear tell of what the geologists think is going on down below, and the trouble they're having out at the climate-station these days. But who's surprised by any of it, really? Only so much you can terraform the surface without fundamentally realigning the core, y'know? And stars above, it's not like we have the resources for a second attempt anytime soon."

She was preaching to the choir, and they both knew it, but she did this so pleasantly that the man held his tongue on his own share of bad news. Even with the ease of her pessimism, he figured it might shock her to learn just how many ending worlds were popping up in the badlands again—each an indication that it wasn't just basic geology fighting back, but that also, somewhere on Maia, fuller pockets of pre-world life persisted, and were sometimes launching little colony-ships of their own into the toxic ether of the human realm. But what good would such knowledge do her, anyway? The man recalled peering into that latest ending world along the crater floor and counting what strange species still eked out a paltry living there. As he scanned the rest of the makerspace, where a handful of local craftsmen were refining printer-plans of their own, and older folks were simply whiling away the afternoon in fuller company, he had to make a concerted effort not to catalog the curious holdings within this ending world as well.

Instead, with a rap on the countertop: "Thank you," he said.

"One hour." She hefted his artificial limb in salute, then retreated into the back.

But the rest of his errands hardly took twenty minutes at the general depot: Medical supplies, food for one man, treats for a full-grown mollusk, calcium-booster for four imminent young ones, and a new energy cell—all from one service counter with a bot ill-programmed for decent small talk. The man debated seeking out a nearby drink and testing the other locals' misery around it, but something about the Oomu's reluctance at the outskirts of town had him turn for the lot instead, a hover-trolley with his purchases tagging close behind.

The man hated when his instincts were right.

Just as he left the main square, he saw large, twisting movements in the distance: The sort that seemed to signal a giant mollusk in distress. His crutch hit the gravel hard as he hastened over to the lot—the trolley whirring frantically to keep pace, while all other bots in the vicinity continued with their oblivious labors. His mind filled with fragments of other confrontations the pair had faced in their decade together: shattered shell bits in a rapid-onset desert storm; gaping under-mass wounds from a confrontation with a stinging mudfish by the coast; and a frightened withdrawal, for months, into the safety seal of its conquistador's apparel, after a particularly vicious run-in with southern poachers, while the man sang to it from the camp he'd made in the outer world. But the scene on arrival instead had the man torn between instantaneous relief and a different sort of fright:

First—The Oomu was fine. The Oomu was *fine.*

Only, the same couldn't be said for the human stuck in its translucent skin.

"MISTER, HELP!" the kid cried. "It's gonna eat me!"

The man swore in two tongues and waved his crutch wildly while shouting at the Oomu, whose tentacles were fully extended and twisted about to observe what was going on along the side of its under-mass. Which meant . . . the Oomu *wanted* this. This was no love-season mistake.

"Hey!" said the man. "Hey, ho there! Whatcha think you're doing? Let the kid go."

But the Oomu only jabbed an accusatory eyestalk at the top of its shell. When the man followed the Oomu's gaze, he saw it, too: their packs torn loose and clearly ransacked; all the safety line's metal parts stripped; and the incubator . . .

Blazes, the incubator wasn't up there at all. The man's gaze darted about, and soon enough found it lying on its side, on the ground.

The man dove for the eggs.

"Hey—hey, mister! I'm dying here! Can't you see that?"

The man watched his hands tremble over the fallen enclosure. Two eggs had been crushed: Their contents lolling in unresponsive pieces, impaled on bits of broken incubator. A third had cracked just enough that the Oomu inside was struggling to breathe. The man eased it from its shell, to give it a chance of transitioning properly to the aerated world, but it didn't look well at all, and sat limp in his hands even after he'd set it free. The man laid it on the ground to recover further on semi-cool stones, then fished around for the fourth. Intact. Cushioned in the fall by its broken siblings. Still waiting to be born. The man shook out broken pieces of the enclosure, cleared the bodies, then set the egg back in the incubator's base, along with its struggling sibling.

Then and only then did he stand to address the kid. He tried to keep his voice level.

"You make a habit of tossing what you don't understand?"

The kid was still uselessly wriggling, as if that could ever be enough to pull free.

"Please, Mister, I'm sorry—I didn't know they were worth something. They're like, collector's items, right? Well, I've got some of those myself, okay? I'll show 'em to you, even, if you'll just—please, this thing, it's going to—it's gonna—!"

The man's arms coursed with a heat he never enjoyed feeling, and all the kid's pleading only seemed to make it worse. He turned to the Oomu's massive head and held out both hands to be tasted: the sincerity on them, and the sorrow.

"You were right, my friend. I should've listened. We could've waited 'til Capitol City."

The Oomu's tentacles swept heavily over the man's hands, his arms, and his head: agreement, distress, grief, and questions.

"I know," said the man, resisting the urge to wipe his face of the Oomu's overly sweet muck. "I know. We've got two of them left, I think. One's not doing well, but it could. It still could. In the meantime, though, please—this one's not much more than an egg for us, too."

"Wait, those're its eggs?" The kid's face fell: the gravity of the offense finally registering.

"Close enough," said the man, his gaze locked on the Oomu's extended tentacles. "But like all Oomu, they carry whole lifetimes of memories. You just killed two full histories of the world before our own, kid. Maybe three. And you've broken the heart of this Oomu, too."

The kid startled both man and mollusk then, by beginning to cry. An arm, a leg, and part of the kid's torso had sunk into the mollusk's skin, but one hand remained to press hard at both eyes.

"Mister, I didn't mean it. I'm sorry. I slipped; I didn't toss it. Honest, I didn't."

"Didn't mean to be stealing from us either, I guess?"

The man was ready for a hangdog look and more excuses, only to be surprised again.

"Oh, no, Mister, one hundred percent I meant to be stealing." The kid was now gulping air to fight back panic. "But just that, I swear. It's hard times out here, don'tcha know?"

The man didn't answer, willing his own breathing calm before extending one hand for the Oomu to take entirely inside its mouth. A trust exercise. Then the man waited, watching the Oomu's contemplative tentacles, while the grind of the Oomu's radula registered along his wrist. He tried not to think of the thousands of teeth that radula represented. They weren't for eating, not necessarily—not with the efficiency of its skin-system—so much as for building: For tool creation, and later use. For snapping pre-world branches into sizes better suited for egg enclosures. For building adult shelters against the worst of the fumes' electric storms. For breaking down large prey into manageable bits for any soft-shelled young to learn how to absorb.

"Even a brute of an adult, you once showed mercy," he said to the Oomu now holding his own bones and flesh in the balance. "This is a child."

And yes, the man was fudging on this last point, and he knew it, for the kid could've been as old as nineteen standards. But what of it? Age-of-majority laws didn't suddenly make sages out of fools, as his own days in uniform had proven well enough. He held firm to this adjusted truth, then, to keep even a flicker of dishonesty from the taste of his skin and the look on his face.

The Oomu pressed down on the man's wrist all the same. It was only a little pressure, a warning squeeze, but enough that the man grimaced: Closing his eyes and running through how much a new extremity would cost him. Then the sensation passed, the Oomu relenting, and the man withdrew a hand coated in denser slime. The man was about to thank it for its understanding, but when he glanced back along the length of the Oomu's foot, he saw that its mercy had only gone so far. The kid was still trapped within its skin.

Then again . . . the kid also hadn't even been a little bit digested.

(The man would've known. The man would never forget the screaming.)

He looked up curiously at his old companion. "What've you got in mind, then?"

But the Oomu gave few answers easily, not even in its more contented moods. Now, it simply curled its forefoot, turned, and started for town limits. The man followed for a few steps, then swore to himself, feeling the weight of the crutch still in hand.

"Hey, hold up," he said to the Oomu. "Hold up! I hear you, okay? We're going. Just, let me load up and . . . and . . . blazes, listen! Listen! Don't you remember? I need two."

He pointed to one foot, then the space in lieu of another, and waited for the Oomu to notice the gesture—which the mollusk did eventually, if grudgingly, before relaxing its own foot anew.

"Wait, whaddya mean we're going?" said the kid, after making the mistake of trying to push off the Oomu's under-mass as it turned. That free hand, too, was now trapped within the mollusk's skin, while the rest was sinking deeper with the Oomu's every move to leave.

"Oh, settle down, kid," the man snapped. "You haven't been eaten yet, have you? No? Well, all right. That's a start." But then, hearing the irritation in his voice, and casting a guilty look at the vivid redness in the kid's eyes, he added: "Parents around?"

"No." The kid choked on more frightened tears. "I'm a podling."

With the mollusk temporarily at rest, the man had had a chance to turn to the controls of the trolley, which he was reprogramming to follow the Oomu instead of him, just in case. But his hand hovered over the input panel at the kid's reply. "A podling? Here?"

His question was met with a despairing laugh.

"Well, yeah. Especially here. You think they could keep this dump together any other way?"

That sounded about right, once the man had turned it over. He couldn't imagine many citizens of a struggling settlement being in the mood to create life by any harder means—although, the downside was that the podling way tended to cultivate less fondness among the elders for the new-forms, which in turn meant a greater hardness, and intolerance, toward all their youthful errors. "Fair enough. So, no one will mind, then, if you're gone—I mean, just for a little while?"

This last part, the man added quickly at the sight of the kid's wide-eyed terror: to reassure the little thief, even if he couldn't tell whether the kid had any right to be so scared.

Only the Oomu knew that part.

"Mister, please . . . please don't leave me here. If I'da known, if I'da only—"

And the kid went on, somewhat incoherently, about intentions and unintended outcomes, while the man shook his head, returned to the input panel, then installed the broken incubator and its contents atop the hover-trolley, carefully penned in by the rest of their supplies. Lastly, he raised his hands to the Oomu's tentacles, fingers splayed, and flexed his fingers a few times to emphasize that he was counting, before flashing a firm ten digits until the Oomu echoed the gesture with its tentacles, twice. They'd trained on this a few times, but though the man knew that the Oomu *could* understand human timekeeping, he also knew that the Oomu was often of a mind notto.

"Ten minutes," he echoed aloud. "Please—just gimme ten, and don't scare him, or they'll all come after you with everything they've got."

At this last, though, the kid's face lit up with another fool idea, so that the man had to whip around and jab a finger in the air. "Oh no, don't you dare. Trust me, if you value your life, you won't call for help. You know how fast an Oomu can dissolve a body if it panics? Do you?"

The fool idea fell from the kid's expression, along with everything but a sickly pallor.

"Okay, Mister. I promise. I won't."

The kid's voice was barely above a whisper now, which inclined the man to take this promise as sincere. The defeat in it, at least, he could believe. He started off to retrieve his leg.

"Only . . . please hurry?"

The man hesitated, his back turned to what now truly did sound like the pleading of a child. A note of compassion, he knew, was called for—but out the corner of his eye, he could still see the two shattered eggs, and the pierced flesh of their contents, drying out on the gravel.

In silence he pressed on.

"Not quite finished yet," said the townswoman. "Just past the mid-calf. Fifteen minutes?"

"Can't, sorry." The man started organizing chits on the service counter. "I'll still pay in full, of course, for your time and the effort."

"Gonna look pretty funny with a half-finished mold."

"It'll match the base model, at least. Always looked pretty funny myself." The man crooked an awkward smile to illustrate his point. "If, ah . . . if you don't mind?"

"Not at all." The woman withdrew to the main workshop, a partition opening just long enough to reveal the near-deafening whir and grind from a series of massive printers. Most, the man knew, were producing building materials. Maybe some were also dedicated to the intricacy of farming equipment, or to barricade blocks to try to keep out the intensifying winds. Either way, only a few would be for specialty projects such as his, along with the fiddly bits needed to keep local machinery in check. Dedicated luxury models, for the use of finer materials and the printing of their potential creations, were for settlements in far better straits.

The woman returned promptly with his half-finished leg, then smiled apologetically while she counted out the chits he'd left on the counter: The half-hearted guilt of one settler's less-than-complete trust in another. The man felt a share of guilt in turn, but only for his own soreness outside town limits with the mollusk. If even humans couldn't manage trust amongst themselves most of the time, why'd he have to go and feel so raw that the Oomu's was even harder to keep?

"Thanks," he said. "Hey, you got a kid around these parts, late teens, podling, the kind with sticky hands, who gets into trouble more often than not?"

The woman snorted. "This one steal from you? Works quick, if it's the one I'm thinking of. Some podlings have the gift in their bones, I think. Want me to call a Monitor?"

"No, no, nothing like that. Only, I figure someone here should know they're with me for a bit, to work off a debt. If anyone asks, I mean. I'll try to have them back as soon as possible."

The woman held up her hands in a say-no-more gesture. "If anyone bothers to report a missing pickpocket and crop-thief, I'll let 'em know."

"*Crop*-thief? I thought the winds were doing that well enough on their own."

"Well, crop-remnant thief, at least. Claims to be preserving the seeds, but we've got servos to sift through the debris and replant the next crop. What in blazes we need special stashes for?"

The man scratched the damp brow under his hat after getting his right limb hitched up again. "That why the kid's going hungry and foraging alone?"

"More or less. Here we work together, or we don't work in the system at all." The woman shrugged. "You know how it goes. What drops off along the way is just nature's way."

Like the beings inside the proto-pockets, or the massive insects that hung about the Oomu: not quite ready to die, but also already lost to the living—although the man couldn't decide if the townswoman's declaration better suited the fate of the kid, or of any settlement so quick to cast off whatever human resources it still had at its disposal.

"'Fraid I do," he replied, setting the crutch down by the counter. "That, I surely do."

Outside, he peered down the main drag of Hector's Haven while adjusting his pant leg over the half-finished mold. No sign of the Oomu having bolted, and no mob gathering in the lot, thank the stars. He walked back quickly but warily, more attuned to the faces nodding in passing, and also to the bots still dedicated to recovery labors. What else could he have said to that woman? If the kid had belonged to someone—been hers, even—would there have been any use to his deliberations as he approached the lot? The terrible heat had left his arms now, but its antithesis, a coolness of resignation, ran the length of him instead. There would be no forcing the Oomu to let go of its catch, and anything less than an instant death blow would see it and the kid destroyed. Unless the Oomu relaxed its hold, the kid was simply forfeit: One life for two legacies. Unless . . . ?

No. No, the man tried to put aside all foolish human scheming of alternatives as he entered the lot, where he noted that the kid was now stuck up to the shoulders of a settlement-issue jumpsuit in the Oomu's translucent under-mass. The little thief seemed calm now, too, but the man wasn't ready to call this an improvement yet. The Oomu's under-mass harbored a narcotic it used to keep its prey from causing damage as it struggled, and probably that was starting to kick in here. Only, the drug alone didn't explain the kid's deeper immersion in the mollusk's skin.

"What, haven't learned to quit struggling? Had to dive in even more to figure that out?"

The kid's reply came sleepy and slow. "Nah, it told me to get in. Easier this way, for travel."

"It *told* you?"

That did indeed sound like the narcotic talking. The man had never put the Oomu's slime to the test himself, but he believed the rumors; and if that drug was starting to affect the kid's perceptions . . . well, it already wasn't healthy for the kid to stay immersed for long, not when a human's skin needed to breathe in its own way, too. He tried to remember if the paralysis caused by an Oomu's toxins was permanent. Too little ever survived submersion in an Oomu for the man to have properly observed its long-term side effects firsthand.

His memory ultimately failing him on this accord, then, the man gave up and approached the Oomu's tentacles—all five of which were out and flexing. Once, twice, and then just two of them.

Twelve.

Twelve minutes.

He didn't know whether to laugh or cry as he set about loading their supplies.

"You're counting too fast," he told the mollusk as he worked. "It was nine, tops."

The Oomu offered what the man took for a shrug, then used its radula to help hoist some of the larger items topside. Soon enough, the man was ready to send the hover-trolley back on its auto-return path, then check to see that the drowsing kid still had a pulse. It seemed strong enough, but how much longer would that last? Hours?

"You sure you know what you're doing?" he said to the mollusk. "This is still a life, you know. Revenge won't bring back the other two."

In lieu of reply, the Oomu tipped the broad helmet of its shell to one side, to help the man climb up again. But the man hesitated now, as the Oomu had on their approach to Hector's Haven. An uncomfortable disconnect was growing between the pair with every turn, it seemed, on this last journey together—and the Oomu surely sensed it, too, because it withdrew a touch to survey the rider, then cast an eyestalk toward the kid and, ever so slightly, allowed more of the kid's shoulders to protrude. Proof that it could let the egg-killer and crop-thief go, if and when it wanted to.

But that gesture of peace also only affirmed, for the man, the immensity of the Oomu's power over both him and the kid, and so he knew that he had to respond to its show of leniency with deep appreciation. Push too hard, demand too much more at such a delicate moment for all three of them, and the Oomu might grow impatient and withdraw its act of generosity altogether. Even now, the Oomu was still watching him, waiting for the expected show of gratitude, and so the man forced a smile in thanks. When the Oomu dipped its shell again, he climbed on—realizing, as he did, that the trust of a human could be every bit as difficult for an Oomu to keep.

The only difference was . . . well . . .

He had to hope that his trust was something the mollusk didn't want to lose.

3. The Oasis

The man sang to the mollusk on the first leg of their journey out from Hector's Haven (Pop'n: 1,416, the sign read after their exit). He knew he didn't have much in the way of natural ability, but figured that the passion with which he offered up Tierra-Prima vallenatos had to count for something. After the second or third rendition of each, he took to interspersing their lyrics with explanations about the human loves they depicted—the old loves lost; the loves one couldn't bear to imagine losing; the unrequited loves; the men who had never found anything to love at all.

Did the Oomu understand the general thrust of any of them? Could the Oomu, with a heart bag used as much for waste disposal as for the free-flowing circulation of blood between organs, ever make sense of the tensions that could strain a human's own? The man had no answer, and no idea even how to pose the question in a way he could be sure of the Oomu understanding—but he knew the difference between when the Oomu was genuinely distracted, and when it was merely feigning indifference: Its tentacles turned away to study anything other than the goings-on high atop its shell. Signs of the latter, in this case, gave the man hope that it was listening after all.

Not that the man was simply resting while the Oomu carried them to Capitol City: Hooked in, he sang and commentated while moving along the shell's central ridge, to set up a nursery for the still-struggling infant Oomu and its sibling (which, for reasons the man could sympathize with, at this juncture seemed content to remain unborn). Building their shelter was delicate labor, with supplies needing to be adjusted to create a "floor" extending out from the shell's ridge, and ballast on the other side; but the greater challenge was doing so while large insects yet buzzed in the uncertain allure of the Oomu's mating-season sweetness. As ever, these hangers-on exhausted the man with their heavy wing-rustle, pungent exoskeletons, and errant scratching of legs and antennae against him. Yet he had his doubts about the Oomu's ability to control its internal biochemistry, and a general fear that the kid might accidentally get digested alongside any potential afternoon snacks—so he tried to swat them away for once, instead of down.

Everything, the man knew, depended now on the Oomu staying calm.

That, and on it longing—soon, he hoped—to sleep.

Sleep, of course, was its own gamble: Half the time, the Oomu retracted fully into its shell to recharge, and this would prove an automatic death sentence for the kid. But since the Oomu had taken such care not to dissolve the thief yet, the man felt confident that it would simply halt where it felt most at ease, slacken along the whole of its exposed foot, and withdraw its tentacles to drowse until restored. Then the man might try to hook his harness into the collar of the kid's jumpsuit and manually ease the rest free—slowly, very slowly—over that sixteen-hour rest cycle.

The man had an inkling, too, of just the place to coax the Oomu to take this snooze. A few hours from Capitol City (the luminosity of which was already tinting the distant horizon) lay a runoff pipe feeding into a pool surrounded by sheltering rocks: Moist, cool, and covered in all manner of succulent algal nibbles. A little oasis with nothing, surely, to drive the Oomu deep into its shell.

It wouldn't be long yet, then. And all the man had to do, for now, was act as though everything had returned to normal between them.

But the Oomu wasn't the only creature in need of settling, as the man realized once the kid had roused to the sound of those traditional love songs, belted high atop the Oomu's shell.

"Hey! Mister!" came that demanding voice from the gliding mollusk's side. "You got anything for the headache your singing's giving me?"

The man paused in the middle of dusting the floor of his nursery with calcium-booster, all the better to fortify the survivors' fragile casings as they glided atop the elder Oomu's shell. He tried to remember the last time he'd had another human along for the ride. Certainly, the moment he registered the kid's voice, he remembered why it had been so long.

"Oh, so now you're a thief *and* a comedian?"

The kid huffed: A good sign, for it confirmed a lack of lung constriction deep within the Oomu's skin. "Attempted thief. It's not like I got away with anything, y'know."

The man shook his head while lifting the infant Oomu into the palm of his hand. Its foot now extended from wrist to fingertip, but injuries sustained in the fall, including that lack of initial oxygen, continued to leave it looking weaker than it should this long after birth. Still, it was eating, so that was something, surely. The man settled the infant in its new nursery, then set a protective covering atop it and the egg, still nestled in the incubator in one corner.

"Well," he called down. "Some might say you got away with murder."

Silence. Enough that the man braced himself on his half-casted prosthetic and peered over the lip of the Oomu's shell. No, the kid wasn't a goner yet. Just busy processing guilt, or maybe trying to figure out a better angle for the rest of their conversation. Either way, the man couldn't decide if he was relieved that the kid had no ready retort for so heavy a charge. He retreated to his saddle and picked up where he'd left off, on the verse that had been so rudely interrupted.

He stopped again when he heard the kid holler something more.

"Eh? What was that?"

"I said," the kid shouted, "Does this guy have a name? This giant slug trying to eat me?"

The man debated the merits of explaining the taxonomy of an Oomu to so ignorant a rural-settlement youth. The thought not only wearied him, but also put him in mind of a past life: The instructional halls where he'd once tried to give lectures, as a field expert, on the differences between Oomu and their pre-species, behaviorally as much as physiologically. He remembered how daunting this task had seemed, with so many eagerly cataloging eyes upon him; and then how impossible, once he'd realized that the students were more interested in his personal conversion from soldier to reclamations specialist. The sheer hunger of those third gens, to know what it had felt like to slaughter so many native lifeforms in service to the "cleanup" brigade issued after the terraform ship's error . . .

Did he still have nightmares from the early hunts? they'd asked him. Did he think his work with Oomu now, or lectures such as this, would ever be enough to make amends?

Just as he had struggled for words to describe the Oomu, so too had the man discovered that he had no language for his first years off the *Ignacio*, which had seen him woken expressly to serve on a task force he hadn't yet grasped the import of. Explain the Oomu? Explain himself?

No, the man had walked away from such failures a long time ago—and into life with an Oomu. *This* Oomu, with whom he could simply be. And so, he found himself resenting the kid's ignorant remark for bringing the whole mess of these pent-up thoughts to the fore again.

Still, he wasn't the one trapped within its under-mass.

He swallowed hard to put his anger to one side.

"Merriweather," he said.

"What?"

The man faltered. This sort of kindness had gone rusty on him from disuse, and he wasn't sure how long he could keep it up. He leaned over his saddle and shouted down: "Merriweather!"

" . . . For serious?"

But the incredulity in the kid's voice made the man feel a touch better. More in control of the situation after all. He smiled indulgently.

"Sometimes Carlos," he added. Then he straightened in his saddle and winked at one of the Oomu's tentacles, which had risen and turned back, all the better to study either the nature of this commotion or why the rider's singing had come to an end.

The kid kept quiet for a beat.

"Okay, Mister, now I know you're just taking the piss with me."

The man shrugged—though more for the tentacle's benefit than the kid's or his own.

"Ask a foolish question," he called out.

"But why's that a foolish question? Is he on some sort of wanted list?"

The man's smile advanced to a snort. "You're really something, kid. Now why d'you think an Oomu even needs a name like the ones we've got?"

"Well, but why not give it one? Give it a name and it'll answer to it, won't it?"

"Sure, the Oomu learn our ways. 'Course they do."

" . . . So?"

"So, what?"

"So, why not this one? He busted or something?"

A second tentacle rose to study the man. The man held up a placating hand, then leaned over his saddle again.

"Watch it, kid. You're not exactly in a position to be calling anything else busted."

"Oh, really? Wow, that's rich, Mister. Real rich. Look, what in blazes I gotta watch for? You wanna talk about busted, you wanna tell me if you've even got a plan to get me out of here? Because here I'm thinking to myself, hey, this is a pretty smart guy, all things considered, so he wouldn't've let us leave the town like that if he didn't have a plan. But here we are, aren't we? Out in the middle of nowhere. And you've got nothing, do you? Unless, like, maybe you're planning to knock this guy out for a bit? Then pull me out while he's unconscious?"

Four tentacles were now turned about to study the man, who had never been much for lying or otherwise concealing truths when they hit too close to home; and who this time couldn't figure out a way to keep flickers of guilt from his face or his sweat-scent. Feeling the heat rise in his cheeks at the kid's words, the man swore in the best language he had for elaborate phrasing.

"Kid, listen, if you know what's good for you, you'll—"

But it was too late. The highly annoyed Oomu kicked into its highest speed: An aggressive zip usually reserved for rare encounters when it saw another Oomu so delightfully bioluminescent that it simply had to dart over and slime-crawl all over the other's shell in fierce, fond greeting and mating dance. The man clung to his saddle and nearly lost his hat trying to stabilize himself without toppling back into the nursery.

"Woah!" he said, scrambling for the light-stick. "Woah there!"

But the light-stick was a fruitless effort to maintain a sense of control he never truly had—as the man knew even as he waved it about and tried to tell the Oomu that it had misinterpreted what it had seen in his face, or smell-tasted from his sweat. Meanwhile, he could hear the kid moaning and spluttering from massive sweeps of air rushing along and under the aerodynamic curve of the Oomu's shell (along with the occasional insect, clod of dirt, and bit of dust).

There was nothing to be done about the kid's discomfort, though, until the Oomu decided to stop—which it did, hours later, ironically at the very place where the man had intended for it to take its much-needed rest. But rather than sinking into a well-deserved flop along the rocks around the runoff pond, the first thing the Oomu did when it hit the cooler, more humid air around the pipe was . . . practically shoot the kid out from its side.

The kid's head hit the dirt before either arm could swing around as a proper brace, while the man scrambled out of his harness and leaped to the ground before the mollusk decided to shake him off, too. The man had just cleared the shell and turned to thank the Oomu for letting the kid go when the mollusk turned all five tentacles and its forefoot from both humans and continued with purposeful—furious—intensity on its way.

Away from the runoff pond and its succulent algal nibbles.

Away from its much-needed rest.

Away from the man, and toward the bright, if hazy lights of Capitol City.

"Wait!" said the man. "The little ones!"

But of course, the infant and egg-bound Oomu would be fine with their elder. Despite the latter's ire, the man knew it would not endanger either surviving youngling if it could help it.

Still, he waited until the Oomu had zipped far enough along that it could be mistaken for a fleck on the horizon before letting his arms fall slack and turning to the curled up and whimpering kid, who was struggling to restore mobility to all extremities. Everything appeared intact, at least.

Next, the man cast about their modest oasis: Willing himself to be calm and look for other positives in the situation. The Oomu was angry, after all, but it hadn't been so angry as to abandon them both at random in the steppes, or to dissolve the kid on the spot. So, maybe the Oomu just needed a moment to cool down. Maybe it would tire soon enough of being angry, and of feeling betrayed, then retreat to this ideal shelter for a good, restorative slumber.

The man crouched to help the kid up.

"Blazes just happened?" The kid groaned, touching a trickle of blood over one eye before trying to clean it with the least-slimy patch on a jumpsuit sleeve.

"You weren't listening," said the man. "The Oomu's got language, ours along with its own, and it hears things. It heard you making plans, and acting like they were my plans all along, too."

"Well, but that's good then, isn't it? Like, that's what got me out, wasn't it?"

The man ignored the question. He turned to survey the pool of murky, algae-laden water, then the slime-trail streaking out toward civilization. Four hours to Capitol City by Oomu was . . . eighteen on human feet, with pit stops? Ten, maybe, if they headed instead for the climate-station that supplied the runoff for this pond, then took a vehicle the rest of the way in?

"We'll camp here tonight," he said. "And then, if the Oomu hasn't returned . . . "

He jutted lips toward the light pollution: a gray-yellow haze in the darkening turquoise sky, at the end of a long expanse of desolate landscape before them.

Even the kid's answering silence seemed crestfallen.

The kid's pockets, at least, proved useful. There wasn't much around the runoff pipe to burn, but enough detritus lined the banks of the little pond to make a fire with the starter on a standard-issue multitool (chest pocket), while a filtration cap (left-leg pocket) helped with clearing some water to drink. Then there was the matter of a nutri-bar (shoulder pocket), which the man declined a bite of when the kid offered; and a dense wad of papers, which had spent the last day secure in the right-leg pocket, but also looked as if it had been through far worse long before.

The man, eyeing each item on removal, regretted that he hadn't outfitted the upper half of his prosthetic with so much as a flask, in case of such emergencies. Then again, as a rider with the Oomu, his shows of helplessness had always been part of their unspoken agreement: No need to get rigged up every day in a jumpsuit like the kid's, when it would only give the mollusk reason to think that he wasn't going to stick around. The downside of unspoken agreements, though, was that the man couldn't say for certain if even ten years of performing relative helplessness for the giant mollusk would be enough to bring it back now. He wasn't even sure it was safe to hope.

He pointed, in the meantime, to the wad of roughed-up papers. Paper was a useful medium in the low-tech expanse between settlements and could be flash-formed easily enough from the right weeds, but the state of Hector's Haven hadn't given the impression of even hemp crops doing well. This was more of the kid's thieving at work, no doubt, though its purpose wasn't clear.

"Love notes?"

The kid snorted, pushing long dark hair to one side with a hand that seemed to have regained full functionality. The kid's deslimed clothes were drying on a rock.

"Nah, look—like I told you, I've got stuff I been collecting, too."

The other hand was still a bit stiff as the kid used both to pry apart a few layers of the pulpy block. The man leaned in, then raised an eyebrow.

"These the seeds you been stealing from your people?"

The kid made a face. "My people are stubborn. They keep getting the bots to gather, store, and replant the same useless things. And, sure, those crops worked for a couple generations—but now we need something more resilient, see? Something with tougher roots, slicker surfaces. Something to withstand all these weird new storms. So, that's what I've been studying, on my own. I've got all kinds of splices back in my bunker. Some of them so tough, you'd swear they could knock back a whole storm itself. The aim's to get a few species to serve as a kind of double-crop—half foodstuff, half natural barrier for the town."

The man couldn't resist a smile. "They still have to be edible, though, you know."

The kid kissed teeth in impatience. "Yeah, yeah, Mister, that's what the Council said, too. So, maybe we adapt our digestive systems, right? We've got gene therapy for pretty much everything else on this dump of a world. Why not that?"

The man leaned back against a bit of protruding pipeline, a thin stream burbling behind him, and knew at once that the kid didn't know how to read the expression on his face. Instead, perched like a wild thing atop another rock, toes splayed and long hair falling all about a scrawny, starvation-bruised torso, the kid peered at him like an inquisitive bird—but with all a human's abiding distrust of fellow human beings.

"What? You got a problem with that? Well, but why not try to change ourselves for once instead of our surroundings? How's it any different than with your leg, y'know?"

The man shook his head and knocked on the half-finished chrome job, impeccable up to the mid-calf. "Don't go bringing this'n into it.

There're those who think I should've laid in and gotten a whole new flesh number for it instead."

"Yeah?" The kid looked at him uncertainly. "And why didn't you?"

The man considered. "Partly, because there's history here. History I don't want to lose or forget. And I guess I'm not sure I won't forget, if I replace the souvenir completely." Then he chuckled to himself. "Plus, time's a coming when the real knee'll give out. I can feel it. So, it might not be the worst thing, to have this old clunker to lean on when that day comes."

The kid was not good at masking disagreement or distaste. "You sound just like 'em, you know. Half the time, I think the real problem with my people is that they love the hardship. Love it, like, they'd rather die doing what they've always done than risk something new, and have it work, and have to give up being so constantly miserable."

The man found himself agreeing with most of this, but burst out laughing at the kid's inference that he was miserable. Age always did seem a kind of agony to the young.

In turn, though, the kid misunderstood and scowled, going hot in the face.

"Well, fine, go on then, laugh while I'm tryin' to talk serious. Wouldn't be the first time."

And the kid smashed the wad of seeds together again, set it by the drying jumpsuit, then curled up with hands tucked under shoulders for warmth, to try to fall asleep.

Amid the kid's theatrics, though, the man had indeed been considering a serious answer—which, yes, included saying how proposing that everyone genetically modify their stomachs was a bad idea in the current culture; but also, that the stuff about the seeds themselves showed a good spirit of inquiry and inventiveness, and reflected the sort of thought processes that the colony could use more of, to bring about the system-wide changes needed to weather coming storms.

He could have said all of this, and more, but the rings of Maia were starting to fill the night sky, and the pair's meager pile of suitable kindling was almost at an end; and as much as the man liked to imagine that the Oomu worried about him when he was out of view, he was now beginning to doubt it: Beginning to wonder, too, if he'd always been projecting his own loneliness and fears upon so dear a companion. And if maybe he was, in fact, a little miserable after all.

Anger kept him silent, then: Anger and helplessness, because if only the kid had kept away from the mollusk in the first place, there would've been no reason for such doubting. If only the little thief had left well enough alone for the—stars, half hour, tops!—that the man had been off buying supplies, then he would've been able to treasure his last night with the Oomu in their usual, relative peace, in an understated communion of silence and maybe song, instead of shivering out here more or less alone . . . and wondering.

Wondering if this first taste of aloneness wasn't just a sign of things to come.

4. The Station

Morning, a poor night's sleep on a twinging back, and the lack of a heavy sweep of greeting-slime across his face, did not improve the man's mood. Frustration, loss, and fear for the Oomu—for all three of the Oomu—twisted in his chest as he surveyed the runoff pond and followed its underground piping in the general direction of the climate-station, carefully dug in at a wide remove from Capitol City. Even this oasis didn't seem so innocent anymore: Nothing did. The more he paid attention to every sign of industry meant to keep the colony going, the more the man felt like they were all close to being ejected from a massive proto-pocket. But if that was to be the end of things for Maia Colony, fine, so be it: What really bothered him was the dithering. Let nature hurry up and knock them all down and out already, if it was ever of a mind to.

He felt a bit better, though, once the kid offered him the rest of the nutri-bar.

And the kid seemed calmer, too: Dressed, long hair pulled back, pockets filled anew. A far more believable profile of a podling long since used to living on its own. In silence, then, the pair filtered more cold, metallic runoff and set out across the remainder of the steppes, surveying the low-lying brush for anything edible: Leaves, mainly, and the occasional root or berry. That silence abided for the first twenty clicks, too, but when they reached formal signs of city infrastructure, including a dirt road heading in the general vicinity of the station (to the left) and Capitol City (to the right), the kid hung back the more the man veered right.

Meanwhile, the man's mood had declined again in the course of their hike. "What?" he said. "Y'think I have time for more of your nonsense? If it's in the city, it needs me, even if right now it doesn't think it does—and all thanks to you. All thanks to all the damage you've done."

But these baiting remarks didn't stick.

"Yeah, but . . . " said the kid, in a soft, flat voice. "I didn't go that way."

The man's nostrils flared. "Did I say you went that way? Did I ever—" Then he noticed the distant look on the kid's face and registered the verb tense. "Say that again," said the man.

"I said, I didn't go that way. I went . . . " And the kid pointed left, toward the climate-station, with half-lidded eyes and in the manner of a sleepwalker.

The man hesitated, then doubled back and rested his hands lightly on the kid's shoulders.

"Hey," he said, shaking them. "You awake? Or dreaming?"

The kid blinked furiously, noticed the man's proximity, then staggered back and away.

"Blazes, Mister! Keep a distance, will you?"

The man squinted at the now fully alert youth, then scratched a bead of sweat down the side of his face. Was it possible? There wasn't exactly a body of literature on the phenomenon, but there'd always been whispers of it, those wild hallucinogenic tales: Of genetic, generational memory that could be deposited, or transferred, to even a human as easily as the Oomu laid sperm and eggs for other Oomu to collect. A consciousness that could extend between organisms even on this side of the atmospheric divide. A system that worked together to keep something larger than itself alive.

"All right," he said, though he was inclined to blame his low blood sugar for the extent of his present credulity. "We'll go left then."

The kid's eyebrows shot up. "You believe me?"

The man shrugged. "Not exactly. But I see now that I should've trusted more in my old friend to have some sort of plan after all."

Even as he said this last, though, the man felt weary: The morning's irritation slipping into grief. Such a waste of their last days together. Such a mess of useless misunderstandings—on both their parts—if the Oomu could've just made itself this clearly known to the man the whole time. Although, if that kind of linguistic clarity was only possible after full immersion . . .

The kid fell in step beside him, shoulders hunched, as they started for the station.

"It does have a name, you know."

The man shook his head.

"An inner one," the kid went on. "It calls itself—"

"Don't."

"Huh?"

"I don't want to hear it."

“No? But it’s a part of—”

The man looked to the sky. He didn’t know where else to look, so as not to snap at the kid again. “It could’ve told me itself, if it wanted me to know,” he said. “It didn’t. Let’s respect that.”

The kid nodded, and this time stayed quiet as they pressed on.

When they tired, they rested—though with care, in the heat—which gave the man time to chew on some decent roots until he felt halfway human again, and then to address the rest of him by readjusting how his leg sat in the cradle of the prosthetic. It hadn’t been used for long distances in quite some time and even a good fit could become uncomfortable under such circumstances, but to his mild amusement, the part that upset him most was how much he found himself missing the original creak: The sheer distraction of the thing. Without it, the only sounds that paced the pair were those of the kid’s boots scraping along the flora, unsettling clods of dirt and gravel, and of the man clearing his throat between increasingly wheezy breaths.

Maybe in Capitol City he could get someone to put it back.

In the meantime, it was hard going. When they finally reached the climate-station, eleven hours had passed—three for stops along the way—and the sheer distance, once traversed in full, left the man puzzling over the underground piping in a less cantankerous, but also far more troubling light. He knew the extent of the system had something to do with long-term plans for planetary stability—a laying of the “bones” for a network of future climate-stations to deflect problems long before they reached Capitol City itself—but the extent of the precaution was itself ominous, when held in contrast with how little such concerns seemed to be discussed on colony channels. He hadn’t seen reports anywhere about the growing number of proto-pockets, either, so either such matters weren’t being discussed because they weren’t important after all . . . or because they were very important, and there was nothing anyone could do that would be worth the chatter in the interim.

Such ruminations dropped clean away, though, when the man saw the low, squat shape of the station in the twilight; and beyond it, just outside its perimeter fencing, a human reaching up to be addressed by a giant mollusk’s mouth and tentacles.

The Oomu’s massive conquistador shell proved a perfectly recognizable silhouette on the cusp of night, and the man’s eyes stung at first sight of it.

The kid, for his part, seemed to be humming vallenatos as they drew near.

• • •

A station scientist was standing by the Oomu as they approached, and when she waved warmly to the worn-out arrivals, the man resented her at once for her proximity to his companion. He stood some twenty paces off, legs planted in the earth while he processed the scene, as well as his own confusion in finding the giant mollusk here instead of Capitol City. Had the metropolis frightened it after all? Had it doubled back for reinforcements?

But if the latter, why here? Why not return to him?

The Oomu's answer, at least to this last, came when it turned tentacles toward him, then away. Oh, yes. It was still hurting. Still grieving the suspected betrayal. The man wanted to rush over and talk to it, explain himself, but felt frozen in place, as if in the middle of a showdown, for how much the woman seemed to draw his attention—and the kid's—to her instead.

"Well," she said. "We were wondering when you'd arrive. Salutations. Stars, you should've seen the look on its face when it sensed this young one coming. A wild feeling, no, that bonding?"

"Sure is." The kid glanced warily at the Oomu.

"Hm," said the woman, with an understanding smile. "Y'know, I wasn't sure if it would remember me, either, but the moment it got close last night, we both felt it—that inner bond. Like it was yesterday, no? Ah, dear one. How terribly long it's been."

The Oomu's tentacles extended and withdrew contentedly, and it replicated a few of the woman's hand movements before offering signs of its own. Signs the man did not know.

Then the woman held out a hand to the man and the kid. It was a long, awkward distance to cross for a handshake, and the woman made no effort to draw nearer to them. Instead, the man had to detach himself reluctantly from where he stood, and take one heavy pace after another, in order to close the gap. At the last step, he almost balked, for the presence of the unresponsive Oomu still upset him so—and then he shook. The kid shook, too.

"Sorry," she said, once they were all together by the Oomu's side. "I'm Leidy. I work climate stats—I mean, obviously, right?" She gestured behind her to the gray stone of a facility entrance, which had been 3D-printed more to bear up to windstorms than to attract visitors. Beneath it, the man knew, lay the real operations hub, with a massive silo, currently closed, that could shoot all manner of thermochemical treatment into different layers of the atmosphere. Doubtless the Oomu had used that very silo to descend and wait out the day's heat: a giant mollusk is something to see, when it went fully vertical at its immense size and weight.

"But before that I was in reclamations," she continued. "I, personally, helped this one with its first transition. Stars, but you were a lot smaller back then, weren't you? Got yourself gloriously fattened up on plenty of desert flies and arthropods since then, I see."

The Oomu glowed—a full-body flicker of iridescence—at this compliment.

And the woman looked the part of an early integrationist, too, with waves of platinum to rival the man's wiry chest hair and laugh lines that also carried their sorrows. Second-through fourth-gen had better ways of weathering this land, but first-gen had been born fresh from the ships, with neural uploads from Tierra-Prima, yet little muscle memory from their base models. Maia had not gone easy on their bodies during that first vital learning curve for the colony on whole.

At the word "smaller," though, the man's gaze darted anxiously to the crest of the Oomu's shell, then all around them. "The youngling and the egg. Where did—are they—?"

The woman made a set of moist popping sounds for the Oomu's benefit, before repeating herself for the others. "You see?" she said, after its tentacles drooped in reply. "I told you. Just a big misunderstanding. He wasn't going to hurt or betray you. He's as worried about them as you were."

The man felt a more concentrated heat blooming in his chest.

"Well of course I wasn't going to hurt or betray it. Honestly, after everything we've been through together, how could you think for a second that I'd—?"

The woman raised a hand against the man's outburst, but the kid answered first, with half-lidded eyes, and that soft, flat voice.

"I didn't think you'd really let me go."

It took the man a second to realize that the kid was neither addressing the Oomu, nor talking about being trapped inside the giant mollusk's under-mass. He looked between the two of them: Surprised, then hurt, by the link that seemed to include everyone but him. "I . . . "

The woman approached him with a clear effort to be gentle. "It tells me that you weren't much of a talker, all these years. Not about anything deep, at least. And it respected that—respected that maybe there were things you weren't ready to tell it. But it took a lot out of our friend, to be with someone like that for so long, even with all the struggles you overcame together."

The man noticed that he was wringing his hat in both hands—and so hard, it looked more like a washcloth. He willed himself to relax his hold, letting the hand fall slack to one side. "'What does that even mean, 'someone like *that*'? Don't you know me? Haven't we known each other all this time?" He raised his free hand to the Oomu, but the Oomu declined to take it into his mouth, to receive the proffered trust exercise. The man let this hand fall slack, too.

"What our friend means is . . . someone who never leaves an inheritance," said the woman. "It's different for their kind. You know that. I know you do. You're still well known for your early fieldwork, you know, even if you've gone to great lengths to try to disappear ever since. I was so busy on the lab side, myself, that it's no wonder we've never met, but even the kids today learn about you. Or at least, from the idea of you. From the stories others tell of your work's impact."

But the man shook his head, not willing to be baited into a conversation about how little he ever stuck around for symposiums, or professional mingling of any other common human type. The barrens, the steppes, the mountains, the valleys: all the spaces in between colonists' grandest dreams of new and far-flung human civilization had always suited him better.

"It doesn't lay eggs," he said. "Never has. Never will. How's that any different?"

"No? Really?" She turned to the Oomu. "Not ever?"

The kid, mumbling as if in a dream, replied in its stead: "I donate my memory to other broods—and like this, with some of you. But what memories do you pass on? What future generations are you nurturing among your own?"

The man stared at the giant mollusk.

"Is that what this is about? You didn't trust me to let you go because I don't share my memories with others?"

"Put yourself in its—ah, foot," said the woman. "So much is blended in the Oomu's world: Past, present, future, selfhood, otherhood . . . If you hold memories so tightly, is it really a stretch to think you might hold other things tightly, too?"

The man pursed his lips, displeased with how reasonable that sounded. "Okay, fine, maybe," he said to the mollusk. "But in what universe, exactly, could I stop you? If I got in your way, what was ever to keep you from swallowing me up, like you did with the kid? Or worse, with the—"

But the man didn't like to mention the other incident, so he cut himself short. Moreover, he could hear the dishonesty in these questions even as he uttered them, for of course the man could stop the mollusk, once they got to Capitol City. The man would be overseeing all arrangements there, and he could easily find the excuse, and the means, to turn the Institute's staff against its request. Granted, it wouldn't be impossible for the Oomu to pursue its plans solo, but it would be much harder. Of course the Oomu had a vested interest in not swallowing its rider whole.

This time the Oomu's response came through alternating tentacles: One extending and receding, then the next, and the next, until all had had their turn. "Maybe so, or not," the signal read.

The woman rubbed the Oomu's tensing neck in reassurance.

"With silence comes a cost," she said to the man. "A rift, which unfortunately it seems this last journey seems to have strained between you two. Obviously, it wants to believe that you'll be true to the decision you made at First Landing. Only . . . "

Shame and anger bloomed in the man's chest, and his incredulity deepened. Had they not broken up whole trafficking rings together? Rerouted a river when Oomu nesting grounds were deprived by a newer settlement? Identified Maia Colony's first serial killer (much as the man had mixed feelings, and sometimes still-haunted dreams, after the Oomu had meted out justice before fellow humans could)? In all that time, had he really just been projecting his own need for privacy and discretion on the Oomu? Could he simply have been more open himself, and then asked his companion point-blank about all the key issues that had built up over the years between them?

Some questions, once framed in the man's head, immediately answered themselves.

And not always in pleasant ways.

The man felt tired, very tired. And foolish.

"Where are the egg and the youngling?" he said quietly.

"Safe," said the woman. "And the second hatched this morning—isn't that wonderful?"

The man nodded.

"And I promise, they'll be safe here until they're old enough to decide their own way to go." She patted the Oomu's shell wistfully. "They're just not ready yet to make the choice that this one has. For now, at least, our dear one must go on alone."

"For now?"

The woman shrugged, avoiding eye contact. "Well, who knows what the future holds?"

But the kid's gaze had long since wandered to the building behind her: Its deceptively innocuous metal door; its low height, and width, and volume. A bunker's entrance. An entrance for those who feared and were preparing for the worst. The kid was seeing it now, too—the suspicions that had been quietly building in the man's head on the way over from the runoff pond. And with that realization, for the seed-thief, came . . . vindication. A spark in those bird-bright eyes, as if it had only just occurred to the kid that a big city would be filled with people more receptive to change.

"Well now, I got a hunch," said the kid with a smirk, "that maybe you do."

But the scientist was unthreatened by youthful provocations. "Indeed," she said placidly, "Still, it's early days yet. We're figuring out better ways of assessing the scope of the situation."

"Uh huh." The man noticed that the kid was now favoring the jumpsuit leg containing the wad of seeds for genetic tinkering—rubbing it restlessly against the other leg, as if to affirm that it was still there. "While towns like mine get torn up in the worsening storms."

The woman's smile turned bracing. "It's neither fair nor just, I know. But our research goes at the pace it has to go. As yours will, too, if you've ever a mind to join us."

Her calmness won the kid over, and to the point of overeagerness. "What, like, *now*?"

"Well, no, not exactly."

She looked to the horizon, and then they all did, listening. The last of the day's light was gone, leaving only Maia's rings and the stars to cut through the staggering dark. The woman turned to the Oomu, her expression changed: a welling up at the eyes, a wavering in her bottom lip, a faltering in her voice. She opened her arms and lay flat against the side of its exposed under-mass: as close to an embrace as a human could manage with an Oomu.

"Safe travels, dear one."

The Oomu slicked her in turn, and she laughed, wicking the slime from her nostrils and mouth before it crusted over. Then the Oomu turned its tentacles to the other two, and after a moment's hesitation, tipped its conquistador's shell to one side. The kid froze, at first.

"You want me to . . . ?"

"It needs you to." The woman clapped a hand on the kid's shoulder. "You hear it within you now, don't you? That need?"

"Yeah, but—why? Why's it gone and put this thing in me?"

And not in me, the man wondered, while watching the rest.

"Oh, no, you did that, not the Oomu," said the scientist. "The bond started the moment you did it harm. That's how it always goes, though in this atmosphere it's not as easy to tell how much our actions create reactions, now is it? All it's done is formalize that memory for you, of your mistakes and their consequences, so that you'll never forget them."

But this answer only deepened the kid's confusion. "Then why've you got it, too?"

The woman sighed, looking past the kid to the man. At last he saw the weight of guilt, the weight of some terrible trespass, upon the first-gen scientist, too.

"Because," she said—to him, more than to the boy—"The Oomu didn't see any reason to respect my privacy, either, when I'd done it wrong. Or, no, let me put it differently—because 'respect' and 'privacy' are such human terms, aren't they?—What I mean is, when I caused it harm, it treated me just as it would another Oomu—just as it's treated you, young one. Only ever once, I suspect, has it really tried to go at this business any other way: to look outside its species standard, and to treat a human as a human would want to be treated instead. Which is an extraordinary thing, if you think about it: The thought of a human who could inspire an Oomu to try to live by his own code of conduct . . . if only for a while. He'd have to be quite the legend, don't you think?"

The man swallowed hard and turned to the Oomu. He didn't need to say anything to be understood; his expression held the question, *Is that true?* well enough. In answer, the Oomu extended three tentacles—the touch-tester, taste-gatherer, and scent-sniffer—and entwined them: the sign for "feels real, tastes real, smells real . . . *is* real."

It sunk in then, for the man, just how hardthe Oomu had been working this past decade, to play the game as much by his terms as possible. And out of . . . what? Respect? Curiosity? A desire to learn humanity as best it could before moving on? Whatever the cause, the man felt a wave of quiet humility, and gratitude, in the shadow of his oldest companion's restraint, though everything about its species longed to merge without consideration for any such bizarre human notions of choice.

And so only at the end of things between them, when the Oomu had most needed to believe that the man would extend the same courtesy to it, too, had it grown anxious and unsure. But why not? Did humans always permit others the autonomy they made such a fuss over for themselves?

"Right then . . . right," he said, setting his hat back over his mop of white curls. He shook hands again with the scientist and thanked her for caring for the rest of the brood. Then, approaching the Oomu's tipped shell with trembling hands—

"Come along then, kid," he said faintly. "We've got one last job to do."

5. The City

The Oomu wasn't as jumpy in the streets of Capitol City as the man had expected—not now, at least, that the man himself was calmer, and no longer exuding all kinds of tense, private, volatile energy that the Oomu hadn't known how to read, or if it could trust. The smells here certainly differed from those in the barrens, as did the obstacles: The cacophony of human-, car-, tram-, and mollusk-traffic throughout the sprawling grid of the largest, most dynamic settlement in all of Maia Colony. But past the towering solar farms and living quarters; beyond the energy stations and research labs; a little further out than the new-builds and the makerspaces . . . there were trees. Massive tracts of city-enclosed acreage for luxury goods and materials, at the center of which stood the immense fortress of the Advanced Biotech & Genomic Engineering Institute.

And inside it, as every colonist well knew: the Zoo.

"Well, old friend," said the man, when they stood outside the Institute's warehouse entrance for trucks and giant mollusks alike. "Here we are."

But he made no move to dismount, or even to begin his very last tasks about the precarious top of the Oomu's conquistador's helmet: To detach the long-term storage rigs, and the sleeping gear, and the saddle. Even through the distraction of heady city fumes, the man was taking in the smell, one last time, of the early heat as it rose off the Oomu's casing; and the feel of scuff marks and healed shell bits within reach; and the sight of what stray insect segments were still being dissolved in the translucent depths of the Oomu's nearby skin; and how the grayest parts of his old friend's shell just barely glinted in the morning light.

And the Oomu knew all this, and allowed it, watching the man without watching him: Pointedly turning all its tentacles in other directions, to make a grand show of giving the man his privacy for grief—at least, until the massive doors to the warehouse rolled aside, and their contact waved from the ground in excited greeting. Then the Oomu glided in, and a whole team of Institute workers thronged about to help the kid and the man unpack the Oomu's decade-long load.

Then, the man knew, it was time for him to go.

The Oomu didn't tip its shell for him—allowing the man one last slide, and leap, and painful protest from a knee of aging, first-gen flesh—but it did so for the kid, who eased more carefully to the ground, then awkwardly turned and patted the Oomu—tentatively—on its under-mass.

"Thanks," said the kid, once the Oomu's eyestalks were watching. "For not eating me."

Then the kid slumped, eyes half-lidded, before regaining full consciousness and giving the Oomu a funny look. "Well," said the seed-thief and the egg-killer, doubtfully. "If you say so . . . "

Meanwhile, the man turned his attention to their contact, "the zookeeper." There was plenty of paperwork to fill out and guarantees to be made, with a little greasing of palms to ensure that the Oomu would be given the utmost care during transition, and only the most up-to-date *proven* gene-therapy techniques—none of this "experimental trials" nonsense to tinker with the formula. Not at his old friend's expense.

The zookeeper then took the man and the kid on a tour of the enclosure, while the Oomu was settled in pretreatment chambers, where the team could gradually acclimate its body to an intermediate atmosphere before it underwent the de-conversion process to its pre-species form. Ten years ago, the science of de-conversion had still been unreliable, but in First Landing, before this last journey out, the man and the mollusk had witnessed news of the Institute's long-term success rate, and of the pre-atmospheric Zoo now being sustained 100% internally, by all manner of reclaimed lifeforms working in uncanny harmony. For the Institute, this was an achievement that would yield decades' worth of new technologies, but for any species that carried generational memory of a time before human trespass, it was much simpler: it was a way back to the world before.

"I imagine," said the zookeeper, once their tour had concluded, and the last payments had been addressed, "That you'd like to see your friend one last time, before we begin."

The man had difficulty speaking, but a nod sufficed, and soon enough he was standing outside the massive medical tent where the Oomu was finally resting—flopped out, in a most ungainly way, after so tense a journey across the barrens and the steppes. The zookeeper invited everyone else to step out, to give the man and the mollusk a moment, but when they did, everything remaining in the tent seemed so light that the man thought it might all, in an instant, blow away.

There were so many things, the man also realized upon entry, that he would never get to ask now, and even more that he could never hope to understand. To think that the Oomu had gone to such incredible lengths to try to live like him, to accommodate him, to allow for his human way of being to subsume its own . . . and yet, had he even stepped out half as much himself, in all that time? Had he even tried to bridge the gap between their species' comfort zones?

No wonder, thought the man, as he crouched before the snoozing Oomu and studied how trustingly its tentacles rested upon the tremendous see-through lump of its head: No wonder that those students, years ago, had clamored to know more about his time as a slaughterer, before he was a helper to the Oomu. Understanding the gene-therapy tools that he used in the field to rebirth other pre-species members was one thing . . . but how many of those bright young next-gens had really grasped yet that some of the most crucial transformations on Maia didn'tinvolve gene therapy at all? How many comprehended that changes in, say, a first-gen's stricken conscience would always come from a far more complex set of forces than labs could ever quantify? And that, if recent settlements were going to stand a chance against coming challenges, they'd all need more such stark transformations of heart and mind before genetic cures could even be considered a viable recourse?

Leaning against the unconscious, sprawling body of his old companion, the man inhaled the pungent sweetness rolling off its sticky skin one last time, and whispered into it: "Thank you, you old lout. I promise, I'll tell them everything. I won't let the guilt go to waste a moment longer."

And then, with a twinge of disappointment—for the Oomu had made no sign of having heard him, or of otherwise being able to rouse itself for its own share of their goodbye—the man rose with some difficulty to his feet and left the Oomu to its long-awaited journey home.

The procedure took eight days and was frightful for the man to follow from an observation booth, where he watched his old friend slowly shrink out of its shell and form a newer, more pliant one in its wake. A magnetic floor in the recovery chamber provided some of the counter-force needed to keep its fragile new body from being flattened during the process, while mild electrical stimuli allowed it to build the muscle responses necessary to adapt to the intense chemical interactions that awaited it in the pre-world atmosphere of the Zoo's main enclosure. There, it would find itself whipped about by dense clusters of volatile fumes while clinging to various floral structures, held together by a range of other faunal allies. It was an existence the man still couldn't comprehend the Oomu's longing to return to, though he tried his best to imagine it in a positive light while waiting. During the transition process, too, the zookeeper would drop in every now and then, to marvel at how strange and resilient these pre-species had been—and how obvious it was why the terraforming ship had not considered the possibility of complex life here when assessing the viability of the planet's brutal atmosphere upon arrival.

The man said little amid these attempts at friendly banter—or when the kid came to visit, chattering away about how the Institute had taken an interest in the whole seed business for frontier settlements; and how they'd offered the kid a place in an internship program where such critical skills could be formalized for the benefit of the whole colony. The man did little at all, that is, except study the Oomu in the middle of its arduous de-conversion—and start in his seat whenever it looked as though the Oomu . . . or rather, the pre-Oomu, its progenitor species . . . was in pain.

Then, late on the eighth day, a supervisor looked into the camera and flashed an "all clear," before a team arrived to take the pre-Oomu, in its tiny enclosure, up to the Zoo. The man bolted upright and hurried to join them in time: the whole team at a minor "airlock" on one end of an enormous viewing window, through which the whirling opacity of pre-world atmosphere could be studied, even if individual forms and species clusters were often difficult to make out in the haze.

The man watched as his old friend was returned in a new form to a more familiar world.

And then he watched through the reinforced glass for hours after, trying to catch a glimpse of his old friend thriving there.

With no luck. No luck at all.

Eventually, though, the lightest touch on his arm startled him, and he turned to see the kid studying him. He couldn't tell if he was dreaming, or if the kid was, or if they both were, when the kid said to him: "Share it all, Mister. Nothing's ever gone completely when we do."

But probably it was just his exhaustion talking, because after what felt like the blink of an eye, the man looked up and the kid was gone. And the Zoo was as impenetrably opaque as ever.

And the world outside Capitol City, which the man faced next, wincing at the sun with his hat held lightly in hand, was a place of more barrens than buildings, more frayed than close-knit networks . . . all of which, maybe now more than ever, seemed in sore need of a bridging of silences.

He set out for the station and its truths.

ABOUT THE AUTHOR

Canadian by birth, M. L. Clark now calls Medellín, Colombia "home." Clark is the published author of science- and speculative-fiction stories in *Analog*, *Clarkesworld*, and *Lightspeed*, as well as in three year's best anthologies, among other publications. Other writing projects include poetry, reviews, essays (especially for a secular-humanist column at Patheos.com: "Another White Atheist in Colombia"), and a novel in the universe of "To Catch All Sorts of Flying Things" and "Leave-Taking."

"Remember The Washington," They Said as They Fed the Ugoxli

JEFF REYNOLDS

They took the baby, swaddled in a blanket made of soft, blue cotton, down the dirt track through vine-covered trees, deep into the swamp. Their boots splashed through puddles as they walked, and insects sent piercing squeals through the woods. The baby slept soundly until the end. Not even murmured conversation about the terrible things that had been done that evening woke It.

Two moons rode over their shoulders as they picked their way along the half-forgotten trail. Little Neid, a red, pockmarked boil shining dim against the night sky. Below it Nolim, fatter and wider, a pregnant blue lady that chased her little red brother like a pool ball across the heavens, features smooth and unblemished this far from her icy surface. Nolim's light was bright enough to show the way, casting the world in blues and grays, with enough of a glow from Neid to make the shadows appear carmine.

When the four men reached the edge of solid ground where soggy earth turned to muddy brown fluid, they tossed It into the waters. It woke then, hissing in fear, but the squalls were brief, cut short by the water that filled Its lungs and the ugoxli with their sharp teeth.

"Remember *The Washington*," three men said, a ragged chorus drowned by the feeding of the monsters beneath the froth. The fourth stood silent.

The men watched the surface churn for a few minutes as the ugoxli took what had been offered, green scales glinting in the moonlight. Once the waters stilled, they walked back the way they'd come, three of them as quiet as if they were in church. Only the youngest of the four spoke, talking rapidly about *The Washington*, the men and women who had died, the rightness of what they had done that evening.

"They got what's coming to all of Them," he said, his right hand making spasmic gestures in front of his body, like he illustrated what he'd do if he could only get within reach of Them. He giggled. "They all deserved what Those got. Them and Their peace. More like fucking slaves is what it is."

"Shut up," the man who had served said. Quiet words, but spoken hard. Like a boulder blocking a path, the words not rounded off by rain and wind, jagged enough to cut.

The man who had served had been among the crews that worked recovery detail after the destruction of *The Washington*. He'd gone out in an old pressure suit that smelled of the previous ten users' sweat, with an Anubis pack strapped to his back, day after day, pulling the dead into the depressurized bay to lay in tidy rows, held to the metal deck plates with magnetic straps. Some were swollen inside their pressure suits, like fat, pink balloons. Some had red flecks staining their face, their last exhalation bloody as their lungs ruptured. Others looked as though they merely slept, statues of icy perfection except for the frost that rimed their eyelashes and lips.

The boy was too young to have known any of the crew who had served on *The Washington*, nor any depravation because of the war. He'd been born after the peace had been offered and folks had begun going about their lives again. He didn't know anything; all talk and not a lick of sense. His mouthy cowardice had taken two lives already, and forced the man who had served to sacrifice a child, too.

The boy cast his eyes to the earth and his talk ground down, words falling away like a pebble sliding downhill, diminishing. He mumbled softly, but since the other men couldn't hear what he said, they didn't mind this as much. He jammed hands into his pockets and tucked his head between his shoulders.

When they reached the main road, the man who had served said nothing. He turned right, heading away from town and toward his home on the edge of the swamp. He walked slowly; eyes fixed on the gravel before him. Nolim overtook her little brother and they traded positions in the sky by the time the man arrived home, the pregnant lady near enough now to overhead to make no difference.

He stood outside the house, little more than a shack he'd pieced together from other homes abandoned by those who'd gone off to war and never returned. The settlers who'd come here to plow and plant and make a new world as green as the old one they remembered, and who gave their bodies to protect what they had started. They floated frozen in space, or rotted beneath the soil of some planet no one could name. He took little pieces of their memories for his own and lived in the shade of their haunts.

After a long wait, he went inside. Not much to see in the one room beyond a worn table and chair, a bed in the corner. He bent and moved a loose floorboard aside. A small bundle of dirty, red cloth lay in the exposed gap. He unwrapped it, picking the antique Smith & Wesson out of the scrap of an old shirt he had used to keep it from getting dirty. He sat on the edge of his bed, thumbing the hammer back, pulling the trigger, listening to the click as the pin snapped on an empty chamber.

He let out a long breath and held his lungs empty as he pressed the barrel against his temple, hard enough to mark his skin. Then he pulled the trigger, each snap sending a jolt through his skull. Once for each of his friends from *The Concord*, killed when she crashed on a nameless world. Once more for *The Lexington* bridge crew, sucked out of their ship when a rail gun slug punched through the room. Once for his brother, lost during a ground landing from the assault ship, *Akoshi*. A last time for the two hundred and ten bodies he pulled from space after the destruction of *The Washington*. Then he took a box of ammunition from the hole and loaded the cylinder.

He climbed into the rude bunk against the wall boards and fell asleep clutching the revolver to his chest.

The man who had served walked into town. Morning light gave a watery glow to the road ahead, and it would be hot. It was always hot.

Someone had found the bodies. He kept an old radio by the bed and charged the battery with a hand winder. He listened to the news every morning. He didn't want to hear it had all begun again, though it couldn't of course, now that the peace had been offered, accepted. He didn't want to know. But he did it just the same, and he'd heard the news before he left the shack that morning.

Some government official had stopped to pay an early morning call on the only members of They who lived inside the colony. He'd knocked and the door swung open. The mouthy boy had told his father he'd closed it after they'd left with the baby, but he must have lied. The official found the bodies where the men left Them lying on the cold floor of Their home.

"They moved, so I shot Them," the boy had said. "They shouldn't have moved. Fucking ugly monsters, that's what They are. I told Them not to move."

The father had called the man who served to ask for his advice. The three who did the killing hadn't known there was a baby and couldn't decide what to do. None of them had the stomach to kill an infant. They called someone they thought hated Them worse than they did.

"He thinks we should leave the kid where it is," the father had said. He shrugged, a helpless gesture suggesting he probably agreed.

"This isn't about what any of you think," the man who had served had said. "You didn't think at all." He didn't like this man, who'd come here years ago on a freighter and had decided to stay. A man with no roots. He hadn't served, but talked as though he knew what it was like. He'd stayed home, got a medical avoidance slip. He'd avoided taking the peace, and kept his son from it as well.

The boy's father had shrugged again. "No, maybe not. But that still leaves us with deciding what to do."

The boy liked to talk. All the walk into the swamp he talked about Them, how he'd killed Them, how it felt. He wanted to kill more of Them. He couldn't still his tongue and be silent in the doing of it, he had to relive it over and over. The man who served had known young men like him, the ones who talked about life and death like they were two sides of a game. They were broken inside, cracked pieces of clay that you couldn't repair, and their fear leaked from the gaps in their flesh like weeds sprouting through broken pavement. Soon enough he'd talk to someone else who wasn't his father. The kid would be reported, picked up, interrogated. They'd have the other two soon after. They'd make them all take the peace, and then They'd come for him.

That he couldn't allow.

So, he walked to town, and the gun rubbed against the skin at his waist where he'd tucked it into the top of his trousers. He didn't have a holster, and that was the best he could do. He kept his shirt untucked to cover it.

The other two men were waiting for him near the first houses, leaning against the side of a picket fence that slumped over. The man who was the father pulled at strips of peeling paint and flicked them onto the road. He heard the crunch of gravel and looked up when the man who had served approached. He nodded at the other man and they stepped forward.

"Rest easy, friend," the father said, lifting a hand and placing it on the chest of the man who had served, as though he could hold him back. As if anyone could hold back the tide. The tide wore you down until you crumbled into pebbles, and then sand, and then nothing.

The man who had served slumped his shoulders as though relaxed. "Where's the boy?"

"Down on the corner at the bar having a drink. He needed something to calm him after all that business last night. He won't talk, you can rest easy, friend." His face took on a sly look, head turned away, mouth crooked. "No one's going to know what you did to that little baby, I promise."

The man who had served nodded. "That's good to know." He pulled the gun out of his waistband and pressed it to the temple of the father.

"Wait," the father said, his voice rising, becoming a whine. "I told you, it's all good. I wasn't threatening you."

The man who had served pulled the trigger. "*The Concord*," he said, as the body fell to the ground at his feet.

The other man stood frozen, his face a grimace, like a mask hanging on the wall of a forgotten temple. Eyes wide, teeth bared, hands coming up in supplication. He shook his head, laughed. He didn't speak. He kept laughing, though.

He'd never served, either. He'd run away and hid rather than go to war. Came out when it ended, took up a life here. The man who had served shot him in the stomach. He waited for the echo of the gun to diminish. "*The Lexington*."

People came out of their homes and their shops. They watched as he walked down the middle of the street and into town, the smoking gun held low by his hip, the muzzle pointing down. They saw the two men he left behind, one dead, one holding his stomach and screaming as he lay on the ground kicking his feet. Some walked back inside, some stood and watched, curious, as though this didn't concern them and, in their unconcern, they were immune to the bullets that sat in the revolver's chamber. Some smiled and waved, as if they knew him. These people had all taken peace into their hearts and heads. Killing them would be worse than feeding the ugoxli.

He left them alone. He moved past them, stopped seeing them. What he saw were bodies lined up on the deck plating. The ones who looked like they were asleep and would wake soon, though they were a frozen block of ice; those he saw most often. They'd found their peace.

He walked past the commissary, the drug dispensary, the greenery, the in vitro clinic. He reached a cross street with a bar on the corner, dirty windows covered with signs, an alley behind it full of trash. The strains of a country song leaked out of its wooden walls, along with the scent of cigarette smoke and beer. Sirens began somewhere, still distant. He had time.

He stepped into the bar, waiting for the dim lights to grow brighter. The boy sat at the end of the bar, alone, tossing back glasses of liquor. His face was in profile, his cheeks damp. His lips moved, silent words tripping off his never-stilled tongue to flow like liquid silk across the stained bar he leaned on. Day-after regrets. The mouthy ones always cried like babies the next day when they thought no one would know.

The kid slapped his shot glass down and wiped the back of his shirtsleeve across his nose. "Another," he said. It was the last thing he said.

"The *Akoshi*," the man who had served said when the noise died and he could hear the music again. He nodded an apology to the fellow who'd have to clean up after him, slapped twenty bucks on the counter, and left. The screen door banged shut behind him.

He turned right, moving further into the colony. The dirt road terminated at fresh pavement. They'd planted trees along this road, shading it with broad leaves. It was pretty. Peaceful. Exactly what everyone had wanted when the war began. A place to live in quiet enjoyment. But who could do that when you closed your eyes and saw bodies drifting through the void, in orbit around a distant sun, like little asteroids?

Ahead stood the low-slung metal building of the port facility, where They stayed. Only Their diplomats came into town, and They were dead. The rest stayed here at Wrigley Station. They controlled access in and out. The ships that landed were guided by Their pilots, the star charts written by Their astronomers, the stargates built by Their engineers.

He crossed the road between cars. A man stepped out of a booth to the right of the security gate. "Sir, may I help you?" he said. He had no weapon but his smile. He didn't think he needed one.

The man who had served punched him. He went down in a tangle of limbs, holding his gut, gasping for the air that he'd lost. The man walked through the open gate, across heat-stroked blacktop, and into the main building of the port.

Inside was hot and dry, with oversized chairs in rainbow patterns scattered around a wide room, a wall of glass opposite the entrance. They waited for him, at least a dozen. The man who had served held the gun at his side. He looked up into Their yellow eyes, black-slitted, inset in narrow heads that rose above slender necks.

"Have you come to your peace?" They asked. None of Them raised a finger pod toward him. They watched him, eyes unblinking, while behind Them, beyond the clear glass, a shuttle rose into the hazy sky of midmorning, its slender, white form disappearing into puffy clouds. The building shook with its passing.

When the sound faded, the man who had served raised the revolver and pointed at the nearest of Them. "I came because it was time."

One stepped forward, or slithered forward, or *became in front* of the others. The man never could tell how They moved, only that They were there, and then here. Something in Their gait tricked the eye so you couldn't quite see it right. This one had more folds of flesh around Its eyes than the others, and Its head sagged on its neck, never rising above spindly shoulders.

He knew Them well enough to know It was old. Maybe older than he. "I served," the man who had served said.

"As did I," It said. "We watched ken go back to dust and more dust." It paused, and lowered Its head to the ground, touching Its snout to the white floor tiles. "We participated in many deaths."

The man who had served had never seen one of Them bow to a man before. "You know why I came then," he said. "There is no peace for us."

"No," It agreed.

"You will take me?"

"Yes," It agreed.

They parted, and the one who had *become forward* now *went behind* and moved toward a wall to the right. He followed, holding the gun loosely, finger off the trigger.

A panel slid open, and they went through. The wet heat of the day grabbed him by the throat, the sweat rising on his skin almost instantly. The heat did not bother Them, it was what They were used to. Across the PDP-covered landing field, a shuttle waited, shimmering in the mirages that rose from the hot stone beneath the diamond-layered surface. A screen of thick foliage blocked the view the spaceport would have of the ocean, and kept cooler breezes from sweeping across the field. He felt like he broiled as he strolled behind the slithering form.

Inside, the compartment felt narrow and confining. The shuttle had been designed for tall beings, spindly beings, beings made of long limbs and many joints. There was one seat, though, for a human, and he took it. He strapped himself into the harness, closed his eyes. The gun rested on his lap, his hand curled around it, as thrust pushed him with its heavy hand back into the seat. He kept still until the pulse of the engines shifted, and gravity fell back down the hole, leaving him weightless.

There were no windows in Their ships. They preferred darkness. They viewed the universe through monitors and screens, text readers that described the world to Them in Their language, slashes and squiggles he'd never bothered to learn. There was nothing for him to see from where he sat other than walls pressing around him. Smaller than his shack, and that somehow comforted him.

It returned. Now the narrow corridors became Its advantage, the rough surfaces of what had been walls and floors and ceilings now all one to It as It *becomes here* from where It *had been there.* It waited until he unstrapped and floated to meet Its yellowed slits.

"How many?" he asked.

"Uncounted," It said.

"*The Washington*?"

"Yes."

"*The Lexington*?"

"Yes."

"*The Concord*?"

"Do you wish Our death?"

He lifted the gun and looked at it. Three bullets in the chamber. More in his pocket. But if he'd wanted to kill Them, he would have done so in the station, when They'd stood before him and waited for him to patch the cracked walls of his heart with the lives before him. That wouldn't have been enough. There wasn't enough blood to fill all the holes he had.

"No," he said. He motioned, opening his fingers, watched the gun drift away in the cabin. It rotated slowly until it brushed a wall, then spun beyond his sight. "I came to find peace."

"There is no peace," the old One said. "We two know this."

"How many?"

"Why do you insist on a number?"

"Two hundred and ten bodies. I spent a week pulling them from space and bringing them home. Seventeen were never found. The took me off the line because they couldn't trust me to kill anymore, but they trusted me with the dead."

The old One bowed to the floor, which had been the wall on the ground. "*The Washington*?"

He nodded.

"How many more did you handle?"

He shrugged. "Countless."

"One thousand sixty-eight," It whispered.

The man who had served nodded again. "I killed men today. They'd broken into the ambassador's home, killed him and his mate. They asked me to help them."

"Why did you kill them?"

"They deserved it. No treatment would cure the virus that infected them, the black stains in their hearts. They didn't deserve peace. They would have left the kid orphaned. But it was my decision to take the child to the ugoxli. It was the right thing to do."

There was a long pause while It appraised him. It lifted its head higher. "You were a captive," It said, unquestioning. "How long?"

"Three years."

"And you learned Our traditions."

"Some," the man who had served said. "The boy thought I was doing what I did out of hatred. Not out of respect."

It bowed again. "You did it to honor Us."

"No," he said. "I knew the baby wouldn't live without the chemicals only its birth parents could produce. But I didn't do what I did because it's Your custom to feed orphans to a predator instead of allowing them to suffer a slow death through starvation. I did it for myself."

"Why do you tell this?" It asked.

"Because," he said, and stopped. He added nothing to that. "Why did you not find peace?" he asked, after the silence became frozen bodies lying on a deck plate.

It turned and made a sound like a teapot whistling. A laugh. "You know why. Some of Us could not find a way to peace. Some of Us decided to stay as We were so that We would be there for you who did not find it, too."

"Some took it."

"But not all. Not even most. Because peace does not mean living contentedly, does it. It means living with the memory of each skin that passed through Our hands but being unable to feel it. That seems wrong, somehow. It dishonors the dead." It lifted Its head high and straight and peered *up* at something beyond the hull of the ship. "I will feel every death that I have made, every skin that I have touched. To take the peace is to dishonor them, and cheapens their loss."

"I'm tired," the man said. "What now?"

"We do what's next," It said. "The only thing left for Us to do."

"I can't go back down there. They'll arrest me. Force me to take the treatment."

"That We cannot allow," It said. "There are other colonies, with others like Us."

It *went forward* and lead him to the control room at the front of the shuttle. When It entered, It turned back to him and waited until he pushed off a wall and drifted down the narrow hall to join. The door hissed shut behind him. It ran a finger pod over the control panel until a green dial appeared. A bite appeared in the left upper of the circle and begin to eat away at the circumference. The circle became a lopsided u, then a reversed c.

It drifted to the center of the room and pulled a strap from the floor. It wound the stiff fiber over Its belly and lay back.

He joined It, finding a spot near where It lay, another strap to hold him down. The c of the circle became a smaller and smaller arc. He craned his neck, watching the light shrink until the last segment flashed red, and then it was gone.

"Are you ready?" They asked.

"Remember *The Washington*," the man who had served answered.

"Always," They said. "We will remember and help others find their peace. Even the uncomfortable peace of feeling."

The engines fired, and they began the long ride toward the system's outer rim and the gate beyond.

ABOUT THE AUTHOR

Jeff Reynolds is a science fiction and fantasy writer from the Maryland whose work has appeared in *Escape Pod, Daily Science Fiction, Apparition Literary Magazine,* and *Andromeda Spaceways Magazine.* He's attended Viable Paradise writers' workshop and Stonecoast writers' conference, and holds a Bachelor of Science degree in Simulation and Digital Entertainment from the University of Baltimore.

Jeff works for Johns Hopkins University Applied Physics Lab, home of New Horizons, Parker Solar Probe, and the upcoming Dragonfly mission to Titan. He's only a software licensing analyst, though, and doesn't do any of the really cool stuff like building space probes and meeting Brian Mays.

We'll Always Have Two Versions of Pteros

DOMINICA PHETTEPLACE

1. Lily 1

Everything was going great until Barry announced one morning that he was in the wrong timestream.

"The wrong what?" He seemed sluggish. Disoriented. In need of coffee.

"I'm not supposed to be here."

The wedding was in three months. There had been multiple disagreements about the dessert platters and the dance numbers. Small fights. Bickering, normal stuff. But there was something off about him today.

"Are you unwell?"

"I'm supposed to be somewhere else."

"Where?" My therapist said that when I feel myself getting angry, I should try to be as curious as possible.

"On the starship *Pteros*."

"But the *Pteros* is gone. All signs of it. You're supposed to be dead and in space?"

He was silent. There was genuine pain in his eyes.

"Why . . . do you think you should be on the *Pteros*?" I asked, even though I knew why. It was survivor's guilt. He knew many of the crew from Uni. His best friend Byrd had been on that ship.

After graduation, Barry had decided not to become an astronaut after all, but a ground-based aeronautical engineer.

"This is not my life." And then he walked out the door.

He didn't even take his briefcase with him.

2. Barry 2

It was Lily, but the wrong one. Perhaps, the other one was wrong too, and all it took was waking up on this side of the asteroid belt to figure that out.

Yesterday, I had been lost in space for more than a year. I thought I wanted to be rescued. It turns out I didn't, especially not like this.

A simple internet search found that in this timeline/alternate universe/extended delusion, whatever it was, Byrd had gone in my place. Byrd, who could be rough and ineloquent, who was all heart. He was the operations officer. In this timeline, he was presumed dead. But that wasn't right. We had somehow switched places and Byrd was the one trying to figure out how to get the *Pteros* back to Earth.

In this timeline/alternate universe/extended delusion, I was alive but felt dead. Yesterday I had been fine, aside from being lost in space. There are worse things than not knowing where you are. Like being certain you are not in the right timeline.

It had been a year since I last saw Lily and I no longer loved her. I needed to get back.

3. Marseille 1

If you put cognac in your coffee, it's the perfect drink for 5:00 p.m. A little cream and perhaps a baguette. I call it breakfast, especially when paired with billiards. I need an unbothered hour to properly wake up, nine mornings out of ten I won't even check my phone. It ruins my concentration.

"Marseille, is it you?" Even at a whisper, the voice was too loud. I dropped my cue, adding to the din.

"Who let you in? Wait, is it Barry?"

Barry. I had some genuine affection for him. We had lost touch and I had thought about going to Byrd's memorial just to reconnect. Late in the day, I decided against.

And now here he was, bursting into my bar in Paris like a man newly released from prison. I was surprised by the strength of his embrace.

"I'm not supposed to be here," he said.

"No, of course not," I laughed. Barry had always been so straitlaced, and heterosexual besides that. His eyes were still dark, keen. They possessed the intensity of a man trying to solve a mystery.

"I need to get back." He explained to me the pain of waking up on the wrong side of one's timeline. It's a high-class problem.

"I'm supposed to be on the *Pteros*."

"Yes, me too!" I laughed. I had been dismissed from Uni for "ethics violations." Depending on your definition of cheating, I had cheated on some exams. It was for the best, it allowed me to try out entrepreneurship. With some gambling winnings, I was able to start up Chez Gabriel.

"You're drunk."

"Don't be rude." I fired up my vape pen, daring him to complain. His puritanism was the thing I least liked about him. I ran a hand through my hair and found it greasy. I hadn't showered today or yesterday. I kept forgetting to.

"*Pteros* isn't gone, just lost. If I can get back on it, I can help it find its way home."

"Something's not adding up here."

"This isn't who I am. This isn't my life."

"What about Lily?"

"We broke up."

At his best, Barry was curious and soulful. Brave. I understood that if he stayed where he was, however one defined "stayed" and "was," he would become increasingly small-minded and rule-bound. And I confess, it helped that he was attractive. I had even remembered a brief period of flirtation before the friendship had begun in earnest.

And yes, I missed space too. Of course, I would help him. But I didn't know how. I invited him to stay the night. He decided to go back to his place.

4. Mario

I wore my human suit clumsily. I thought an Italian accent would make me sound less strange. I was hungry and thirsty all the time, so I manifested a corner café out of space-time fabric. I wanted to spy on Barry, so I put the café on the bottom floor of his building.

He came in disoriented that first morning. I made him a cappuccino.

We're not really supposed to meddle, but it happens. And you can't usually go backward and undo what's done, but sometimes you can.

"I forgot my apartment number," he said to no one in particular.

So I told him. He didn't seem at all surprised that I knew.

"I need to get back." Then he broke down into tears.

So I peeled off my face, just for a second. Just to stop him from crying. Just so he would believe me. And I told him what happened. And then I told him how to make it right.

5. Marseille 2

Barry appeared at my door in the middle of the night.

"I just got back from the wrong timeline."

And then he kissed me.

I had assumed he had dreamed of me. I asked him after. But he said no, it wasn't that. He dreamed of another timeline. Only it wasn't a dream, it had really happened.

"Do you remember Byrd? From Uni?"

"Sort of, not really." But in the dark silence I thought about it some more. Blue polo shirt. Acoustic guitar. An average, alright guy, if I was thinking of the right person.

"In the other timeline, Byrd took my place on *Pteros*."

"So in the other timeline, he's in my bed?" I laughed at my own joke. Barry didn't join in, and I felt bad.

"Are you sad to be back here?" I asked. A wormhole accident had put us three hundred lightyears away from home with only fifteen lightyears worth of fuel. We'd probably never make it back, and if we did, everyone we knew back on Earth would be dead.

"The other place . . . It didn't feel real to me."

"And this does?"

Instead of answering he kissed me again. The affair lasted four years. The friendship continued even after the sex stopped. It took six years, but we found an alternate fuel source and a shortcut home. We were back within a decade of our departure.

Once we returned to Earth, we were put in quarantine. Barry called his parents first thing and then Lily.

She was joyful. Tearful. Just so happy to hear from him. She had thought he was dead. She had given up hope. Despair had led her to a long chain of decisions. Now she was married to Byrd, who had become an engineer and not an astronaut after Uni. They were expecting their second child.

6. Lily 1

There are aliens everywhere on Earth, but they don't always identify themselves as such, at least not right away.

My barista wore a name tag that said Mario, though he never answered to that name. He made the most delicious oat milk matcha lattes and drew incredible designs in their foam. Futuristic cityscapes with meteor showers and flying cars. It was only later that I realized he was drawing his home planet.

He congratulated me on my engagement the day after, even though I wore no ring.

"How did you know?" I thought: he's a stalker, he's in love with me. My heart raced and I scanned for the exits.

"The accident was my fault."

"What accident?" I said, backing away.

"The one that brought the wrong Barry to this timeline."

It had been two years since Barry abruptly walked out of my life. He had disappeared entirely. Enough time had passed that I still thought about what we used to be from time to time. But I had moved on. That's what normal people did.

"How do I know you're telling the truth?" I was standing in the doorway of the exit, ready to blow my rape whistle at any minute.

He shrugged.

"I want proof or I'm calling the police." Barry had made fun of my tendency to turn to law and order in times of conflict, called me a Karen. Further proof we weren't right for each other. I needed a man who understood that sometimes you have to go to the law. Sometimes there's no other way.

Mario's facial features rearranged themselves on his face in the manner of Picasso. Two eyes on one side, where his mouth was supposed to be. Then he righted himself. My cortisol levels were through the roof.

"Are you registered?" My least favorite thing in the world was undocumented aliens.

"I am. I just wanted to apologize about Barry. The whole thing was poorly handled. On my part."

"Where did he go?"

"Back to his timeline."

"How?"

"We were running an experiment. Ill-fated. We don't know where he is, he probably doesn't exist anymore. We thought if we could bring in another Barry, from another timeline, that could make it better, but it just made it worse."

"You killed my Barry?" A homicide. I had a feeling this was beyond the purview of the SFPD. FBI? Space Force? I didn't have those agencies on speed dial, I'd have to look them up.

"Probably. It was an accident."

"You owe me."

"I do," he said.

Yet he never paid up. He disappeared. Space Force investigated my account, but came up with nothing. They seemed to think I was making the whole thing up. Barry's disappearance was never solved.

The *Pteros'* homecoming moved me. I wasn't ready for it, but seeing the crew disembark brought tears to my eyes.

I went to the post-quarantine parade. Clubbed at the after-parties. When I got home, I saw that I had missed a call from Byrd. I called him right back. He was still up.

"I'm sorry about Barry." He offered his condolences and I accepted. Later he came over to pay his respects. He didn't start formally courting me until the next year. Every time something good happened I wondered if Mario had used alien magic to intervene on my behalf. A promotion. A rainbow. My engagement to Byrd. My first pregnancy had been difficult and at one point I shouted at the sky that if my girl came out healthy, we could call ourselves even.

She did. And so we are. I think. I'll never know for sure, because in addition to all the blessings he may or may not have bestowed, he did me the favor of never showing any of his faces to me again. At least not in this timeline.

ABOUT THE AUTHOR

Dominica Phetteplace writes fiction and poetry. Her work has appeared in *Zyzzyva, Asimov's, Analog, F&SF, Lightspeed, Copper Nickel, Ecotone, Wigleaf, The Year's Best Science Fiction and Fantasy,* and *Best Microfiction 2019.* Her honors include a Pushcart Prize, a Rona Jaffe Award, a Barbara Deming Award and fellowships from I-Park, Marble House Project, and the MacDowell Colony. She is a graduate of UC Berkeley and the Clarion West Writers Workshop.

History in Pieces

BETH GODER

Puzzle Piece 37

Cassandra steps onto the surface of the planet, her insulated boots making soft indentations in the dirt. The fan that keeps her spacesuit from overheating whirrs over the harsh cadence of her breath.

She doesn't see the Archivists, but they are already documenting, building the record that will express this historical moment, a series of interlocking puzzle pieces filled with visual, empathetic, and sensory images.

Archivist Tan places an unformed puzzle piece in his gripping bones, channeling the emotions of Cassandra, who feels a sense of wonder and hope and fear. The puzzle piece melts, then reforms, shaped by Cassandra, although she does not know it.

Puzzle Piece 42

Nine humans sit around a table bolted to the floor of their spaceship.

"We're going to be rich," says Josef, his gray hair gleaming in the artificial light. He has been on many survey missions, but never to a planet as plentiful as this one, with flowers that produce a nectar sweeter than sugar, with rivers of liquid gold.

Desire flows off the humans like oil, like the golden rivers with their hidden depths. Josef wants to take sanctuary in wealth, finding the safety he has been missing all his life. Cassandra wants to be famous for her discovery; the money will only be one facet of her greatness. Aviva wants to prove she is better than her siblings; any status symbol will do—prestige, money, scientific recognition. Some of the humans only want the money for the wanting of it, a desire inchoate and overpowering.

They still have not found the Archivists, but they have not looked very hard.

Puzzle Piece 12

The human ship is descending quickly. Archivist Tan wonders what strange creatures will come this time, if their memories will be as virulent as those who have come before. He wonders what their feelings will taste like.

The prismatic puzzle glows in the sun's weak light. Archivist Tan slots puzzle piece 12 into place, his memory of this landing, so that other generations can know what he knows.

Puzzle Piece 201

Josef has been dead for two weeks. Archivist Tan can taste Cassandra's grief, and it is tinged with some deeper bitterness, like a root left too long underground.

Puzzle Piece 60

Josef hikes in the weed forest, where a bridge crosses a vast, golden river. Josef touches the interlayered braid of the bridge cable. He realizes it is a made thing.

Archivist Tan stands at the end of the bridge.

At the sight of the Archivist's many bones, Josef loses his footing and almost falls into the liquid below, but catches himself. Archivist Tan can feel Josef's fear and wonder.

Tan holds out a puzzle piece. It represents the first part of the humans' journey, which Tan has documented fastidiously. Josef backs away. Seeing nowhere else to go, he jumps into the river, not hearing Tan's warning. *Fatal water.*

The golden liquid eats through Josef's spacesuit, down to his shining bones.

Puzzle Piece 61

Josef's bones, licked clean by the river, deposited at the spaceship hatch.

Is this the correct funerary rite? Archivist Tan doesn't know. The humans have many conflicting memories.

Puzzle Piece 674

Archivist Tan places his thoughts into the mutable, fragrant substance: Will future Archivists build this puzzle in a linear way, trying to reconstruct the shape of the past, or will they clasp the pieces that glow most strongly, scooping out singular moments from the flow of history? It is so easy for pieces to become lost, to disintegrate. What sort of history is a fragmented history?

Puzzle Piece 70

Aviva has always been an explorer. Josef's death does not stop her.

She climbs mountains with crystal adhesions. Walks the twenty-two kilometers of a valley bright with seafoam. She is the first to take off her suit and breathe the air, which tastes faintly of salt.

Archivist Tan wants to contact her, but she is immersed in the glory of her discoveries. Instead, he uses the mutable substance to capture her wonder and pride, her ambition and energy.

Puzzle Piece 300

Cassandra takes a puzzle piece from Archivist Tan. She sees the Archivists in their long lines, worshiping order and chaos, eating the blue twisted stems that grow underneath the ground. She searches for the next piece to connect, and all over the planet, the Archivists feel a corresponding tremor, for they too love order and completion.

Cassandra is overcome with wonder and hope and a wide, unquenchable awe.

In this true moment of first meeting, Cassandra accepts what the Archivists have offered—a living piece of history, which will be transmuted in her hands, shaped by her choices, her thoughts, the wide possibilities of the future.

Archivist Tan gently takes the puzzle piece with his gripping bones. Together, they hold the fragrant substance between them, creating a fused memory of many parts.

Puzzle Piece 362

Aviva runs in the seafoam valley, turning her anger into motion. She will not speak to the Archivists or grasp their gripping bones like Cassandra. Doesn't Cassandra know that the Archivists are recording them? Can Aviva recuse herself from this historical record?

Puzzle Piece 800

Cassandra frantically boots up the autopilot. Too late. She falls over the console, blood brimming from her ears, purple welts across her face.

Archivist Tan tempers his grief in silence, twisting it upon the forge of his mind to see how it will break.

He crushes a purple mushroom in his gripping bones. It is an irrational action. Archivist Tan crushes a field of mushrooms, stomping with his largest bones, although it hurts his cracked side.

The spores that settle on him will not hurt him. How long had those spores settled on the bodies of the humans, waiting to bloom?

Puzzle Piece 473

Cassandra touches Tan's gripping bones. They drink together from the same cup, for water is life for both peoples, despite their physiological differences. Tan communicates with Cassandra through the mutable substance of the puzzle. He thinks that she may stay.

His hope is like the rushing of a golden river, swift and powerful. Dangerous. Between their differences, they have found a space to exist together. They tell each other stories, sharing memories—her childhood on a farm stretched beneath a yellow sun; his first Archival Passage, where he rubbed the mutable substance all over his bones and did not disintegrate. Her mind contains a balance between order and chaos—he wishes his own thoughts could obtain this unsortable quality.

Purple mushrooms frame their camp. Now that the wet season has come, many varieties have sprouted from the dark dirt.

Cassandra picks a mushroom. Absently, she tosses it from hand to hand. Archivist Tan is amazed by her dexterity.

Through the mutable substance of the puzzle piece, he says to her, *I am sorry.*

What he is apologizing for, he does not know. Perhaps that he can know and taste and feel her emotions and the surface of her thoughts, which he knows disturbs her. He cannot turn off this sense, any more than she could stop feeling the wind on her skin. Perhaps he only wants her forgiveness for whatever is to come.

The past spools out behind them. The future is a long road they must walk.

Instead of forgiveness, she touches the bone that runs along his left side, with the crack down the middle. *Tell me how this happened*, she says, and so he describes the sinking valleys of Ivalthe and the three-toed beasts that roam there, and the journey he took when youth was fresh upon him and the world looked new.

Puzzle Piece 788

A strange fungus has overtaken Aviva, working its way into the crevasses of her spacesuit. Purple welts form on her arms. Blood brims from her ears.

Puzzle Piece 1005

The humans are dead. Their ship sits like a toothless mouth, yawning open, crawling with fungal spores. An unintended monument.

The mutable substance holds their memories. Which amber thoughts will persist? Which will crumble? Who will read this fragmented history and know something of this past?

Puzzle Piece 1006

Archivist Tan makes a copy of the record, 1006 interlocking puzzle pieces, and sends it into space, following the trajectory the human ship made. The original is shelved in the underground archive of Balthanos, waiting for gripping bones. Or hands.

Archivist Tan thinks he will go again to the valleys of Ivalthe. There, he will bury the puzzle piece he has kept close. Not everything belongs in the historical record, to be scrutinized and examined. The past must keep some secrets.

Puzzle Piece 1

It is only this: a ship in the sky, radiating hope, bringing the unknown future.

ABOUT THE AUTHOR

Beth Goder works as an archivist, processing the papers of economists, scientists, and other interesting folks. Her fiction has appeared in venues such as *Escape Pod, Fireside,* and *Flash Fiction Online.*

Peter Pan Through the Years

CARRIE SESSAREGO

"All children, except one, grow up." These words open the novel *Peter Pan*, by J. M. Barrie. The story was published in and takes place in Edwardian England (after the death of Queen Victoria and slightly before World War I). Its pages are full of adventure, playfulness, terror, and levity. The novel was one of several versions of the story by author J. M. Barrie, and dozens of versions by others followed and continue to be made through the generations. Why do we keep retelling this story?

J. M. Barrie, the author of *Peter Pan*, was famous during his lifetime for his books and plays even prior to *Peter Pan*. Barrie liked to take his dog to Kensington Park for walks. There, in 1897, he befriended boys George and Jack Llewelyn Davies. Barrie and the boys' mother, Sylvia, became close friends. Their father, Arthur, was more ambivalent about Barrie's incessant presence in their lives but tolerated the friendships. The Barrie and Llewelyn Davies families soon became inseparable, seeing each other almost daily and going on vacations together.

The first appearance of Peter Pan came in a book for adults called *The Little White Bird*, published in 1902. Barrie loosely based the book on his relationship with George Llewelyn Davies. In the book, the narrator tells a child a story about an infant Peter Pan who lived in Kensington Gardens. This was a story that Barrie told George about George's baby brother, Peter. Later, Barrie expanded the character to become the Peter Pan modern readers recognize. He told the boys:

> *"I suppose I always knew that I made Peter by rubbing the five of you violently together, as savages with two sticks produce a flame. I am sometimes asked who and what Peter is, but that is all he is, the spark I got from you."*

In *The Little White Bird,* Peter, who, like all babies, is part bird, flew out the window. He is only "seven days old" and spends his time in the park, where nannies often bring their charges. Eventually he goes home only to discover that his mother has had another baby and forgotten him. Heartbroken, he returns to the gardens where he lives with birds and fairies.

While the book was written for adults, the chapters about Peter were rereleased as a children's book called *Peter Pan in Kensington Gardens.* After the popularity of *The Little White Bird,* Barrie changed and expanded the character of Peter Pan into an older child who lives in Neverland. In 1904, Barrie wrote a play called *Peter Pan: or, The Boy Who Wouldn't Grow Up,* and he rewrote the story again for the play *Peter Pan and Wendy.* A novel, *Peter and Wendy* (sometimes published as *Peter Pan*), was published in 1911.

Countless stage productions followed through the decades. From the very first productions, Peter has traditionally been played by a woman, and the same actor plays both Captain Hook and Mr. Darling. In 1954, Jerome Robbins produced and directed a musical version, starring Mary Martin as Peter. This version has been presented on television and on both large stages and tiny community theaters countless times since. In testimony to the lasting appeal of the 1954 musical, a slightly updated version of the same musical was performed live on television in 2014. The musical has endured as a favorite production among schools and community theaters not only because of its energy and catchy music, but also because it contains a large ensemble cast including many roles for children and, other than the flying apparatus, can be produced cheaply, a perfect marriage of practicality and artistic merit.

In addition to the stage plays and musicals, *Peter Pan* has been made into or inspired numerous movies. The first film version was a silent film, released in 1924. Disney released its animated musical in 1953, cementing specific images of Peter Pan, Hook, and Tinkerbell in the imagination of modern audiences. Recent film adaptations include *Pan*, released in 2015, and *Wendy*, released in 2020. Additionally, many versions that either retell the story or are inspired by elements from the story have been made for television or have been produced directly for the home viewing market, including the *Disney Fairies* franchise.

For J. M. Barrie, *Peter Pan* had different meanings depending on which version he was writing. Starting with the 1904 play, the plot was always the same, but different lines were added or cut. For instance, when he discovered that children kept hurting themselves by trying to fly with the power of Happy Thoughts, he added fairy dust to the list of requirements for flight. When WWI was underway, the line "To die will be an awfully great adventure" was cut by many theaters, as the idea of a gallant death in battle was replaced in the public eye by images of poison gas and trenches.

Reading the 1911 novel *Peter Pan* today can be a jarring experience by today's expectations. The gender roles are ironclad. Wendy offers to return to Neverland with Peter yearly, not for adventures, but "to do his spring-cleaning." Adults and children are killed off willy-nilly. The Native Americans are described exactly the way an Edwardian English child would picture them, which is to say, not in ways or with terms that would be remotely acceptable today. The Darlings employ Liza the maid, who is sometimes allowed to participate in family "romps." Liza is assumed to be around ten years old. Liza does not get to go to Neverland.

The fact that there are so many characters in the book and the fact that the story is deliberately made simple and open-ended means that writers can approach the story through many characters' eyes and through many viewpoints, emphasizing, or exploring different aspects of the deceptively simple plot, sometimes through a more modern lens. For instance, in *Wendy*, a film from 2020, a modern-day Wendy and her brothers follow Peter Pan in a story that focuses on Wendy's viewpoint and allows Wendy to be just as rough and tumble as the boys while also addressing the specific challenges that girls face in adulthood. In 2020's *Come Away*, Peter and Alice (as in *Alice in Wonderland*) are siblings who use fantasy to cope with real-world loss. The movie contrasts coping skills that Alice and Peter possess with each other (Alice is happy to go back and forth between reality and fantasy, but Peter is not), and with the coping skills of their parents.

Some versions are clearly aimed at young children and attempt to reflect a more ethnically diverse and feminist worldview. These include TV shows (*Jake and the Never Land Pirates*, the *Disney Fairies* franchise), movies (*Hook*, from 1991, and *Pan*, from 2015), as well as novels, such as the *Peter and the Starcatchers* series by Dave Barry and Ridley Pearson. These are stories that try to maintain the adventurous tone of the original while being more in tune with the social mores of today—more feminist and less stereotypical in the portrayal of Native Americans. While they may not succeed in achieving their goals (*Pan,* for instance, became notorious for casting a white actress as Tiger Lily), they are clearly trying to resonate with modern children, or at least modern parents. Such versions for children emphasize the "carefree, magical land of adventure" aspect of the *Peter Pan* story.

Meanwhile, today's sense of unease regarding issues like sexuality, the darker implications of "never growing up," and a fascination with villains has led to some horror-based homages and experiments in role reversal, usually intended for adult audiences and readers. The novel *Lost Boy: The True Story of Captain Hook* by Christina Henry portrays Peter Pan as a sociopath and Neverland as a violent world. Another novel, *The Child Thief* by Gerald Brom, depicts Peter Pan as a kidnapper who turns children into child soldiers. The graphic novel *Lost Girls* by Alan Moore uses the idea of Wendy following a charismatic boy to a secret destination as a way to explore female sexuality. The television show *Once Upon a Time* casts Peter Pan as the antagonist, focusing on his selfish, arrogant, and sadistic qualities, and depicting Hook as an (eventual) hero.

The plot of *Peter Pan* can be summed up in simple, broad strokes: Peter takes the Darling children to Neverland, they have adventures, and although they return home, Peter stays in Neverland, vowing to "never grow up." However, thematically *Peter Pan* is complex, which is part of why it endures. It works as adventure, as fantasy, as allegory, and as horror in different hands because the original story contains elements of all these things.

Superficially, the novel *Peter Pan* promises eternal youth with no consequences (to Peter). For Peter, no grief is lasting because he forgets events right after they happen, not to mention the fact that he is relentlessly self-centered. Peter forgets his adventures soon after they take place, so he never knows grief, or nostalgia, or boredom, and he can't learn and thus mature. He's not an old soul in a young body, like a vampire. He's truly forever physically and mentally young, and he still has "all his first teeth." He has no empathy and therefore he does not understand suffering. The other children understand concepts of death and of cause and effect, but Peter does not. He lives in an eternal Now and sees only himself.

Even the children who run off with Peter don't worry much about the consequences of their actions. They are sure that the mothers on the Mainland are always waiting with the window open—all but Peter's, and Peter finds an unending chain of replacement mothers when he wants them, by befriending Wendy and her generations of daughters. The narrator of the book, who talks directly to the reader, is often wishing the children would face real consequences, but they never do:

> *Off we skip like the most heartless things in the world, which is what children are, but so attractive; and we have an entirely selfish time; and then when we have need of special attention we*

nobly return for it, confident that we shall be embraced instead of smacked.

And yet, despite the superficial appearance of a lack of consequences, *Peter Pan* does suggest that life on Neverland comes with a cost. Peter suffers from terrible nightmares. Hook lives in a constant state of agonized terror, with a desperate sense of inadequacy. The Lost Boys are often hungry and have to worry that Peter will "alter" them or "thin them out." A startling number of people die bloody, violent deaths in the original book's pages.

When Wendy is reunited with her mother, Peter cannot join in: "He had ecstasies innumerable that other children can never know; but he was looking through the window at the one joy from which he must be forever barred." This hints at an underlying emptiness within Peter. His relationships are (to him) without the threat of lasting pain (because of forgetfulness and lack of empathy). But that also means that all of his relationships must, on his side, be shallow ones. One cannot know real love if one is not willing to experience real pain.

Because the novel presents a world of adventure and fun with a total lack of consequences on one level and a nightmarish, violent world of terrible consequences on another, *Peter Pan* can be read in many different ways. The novel itself alludes to the contradictory nature of Neverland:

Of all delectable islands the Neverland is the snuggest and most compact . . . When you play at it by day with the chairs and tablecloth, it is not in the least alarming, but in the two minutes before you go to sleep it becomes very nearly real. That is why there are nightlights.

Just as Neverland is at once utopian and terrifying, "never growing up" carries promise and menace. Growing up can be scary. It is unknown territory. To some, it sounds restrictive and dull. Puberty can be miserable, and junior high school even worse. Old age can seem horrifying. Modern versions of *Peter Pan* are able to continue to explore the fear of growing up because for many that fear has never gone away. For instance, in *Wendy*, the children are afraid that they will have to give up their dreams and be blue collar workers and parents, like their mother, just as Peter Pan, in the original novel, dreads having to one day work in an office.

By the same token, a lot of children never grow up. For instance, we can use that term to describe children who, like the Lost Boys, go missing and are never found or those who die young. We might use that description for people who age physically, but remain narcissistic and profoundly emotionally immature, as in the nonfiction book *The Peter Pan Syndrome*. In fiction, the movie *The Lost Boys* (1987) uses the phrase as its title to apply the sense of mystery and disappearance to missing children who become vampires. In two tragic real-world examples, "the Lost Boys" has been used to refer to the boys kicked out of a polygamous sect in Utah to make more girls available for the older men to marry. Robert Kolker also evokes this sense of unresolved loss by titling his nonfiction book about murdered sex workers *Lost Girls* (later made into a movie of the same name).

Why do we keep retelling the story? Because every generation of adults includes those who fear losing their children and every generation of children has those who fear losing their childhood. Every generation also includes people who see the darker side of never growing up, and what that actually entails. *Peter Pan* serves every audience because, in its different characters and the voice of the narrator, it is written to appeal to our most primal instincts—the desire to be free from all responsibilities, the desire for adventure, the desire to have a purpose in life, the desire to be respected, the desire to be taken care of or to take care of others, the desire to live and grow. Neverland can be scary, or it can be fun, depending on whether the night-lights are off or on. The story goes on, "as long as children are gay and innocent and heartless."

ABOUT THE AUTHOR

Carrie Sessarego is the resident "geek reviewer" for *Smart Bitches, Trashy Books,* where she wrangles science fiction, fantasy romance, comics, movies, and non-fiction. Carrie's first book, *Pride, Prejudice, and Popcorn: TV and Film Adaptations of Pride and Prejudice, Wuthering Heights, and Jane Eyre,* was released in 2014. Her work has been published in *Interfictions Online, Pop Matters: After the Avengers, The WisCon Chronicles Vol. 9, Invisible 3, Clarkesworld Magazine,* and two volumes of *Speculative Fiction: The Year's Best Online Reviews, Essays and Commentary.* She spends her time wrangling her husband, daughter, dog, and three cats.

Thrilling to the Harmony: A Conversation with Karen Osborne

ARLEY SORG

As a self-avowed *Star Trek* nerd, it is perhaps fitting that Karen Osborne's earliest attempts at selling fiction were in the *Star Trek* franchise: "As a teen, I once wrote a *Star Trek: Voyager* spec script with a friend over CompuServe, which became my first real rejection letter. It's framed."

Osborne's first SFF sales of "Retirement" to *Aoife's Kiss* and "Gazer" to *Electric Spec* may have flown under the radar. But she landed in pro markets with 2017's "An Equal Share of the Bone" in *Escape Pod*, which was listed as "Notable" in *The Best American Science Fiction and Fantasy 2018*. Reviewers took notice, and as her work appeared in more pro venues, such as "The Bodice, the Hem, the Woman, Death" in *Beneath Ceaseless Skies*, her name appeared ever more frequently in short fiction review columns. Short story "The Dead, In Their Uncontrollable Power" in the March/April 2019 *Uncanny* earned her nominations for both Nebula and Sturgeon awards. Debut novel *Architects of Memory* began her Memory War duology, launched September 2020 by Tor Books. Reviewer Liz Bourke described it in her *Locus* column as "a very entertaining book and a debut with a lot of promise for the rest of Osborne's career." Book two, *Engines of Oblivion*, is due February 9, 2021.

Karen Osborne was born in Niskayuna, NY near Schenectady. She graduated from Niskayuna High School in 1998 and went to college at Nazareth College in Rochester, NY, where she studied English, communication and information design. She worked for community weekly newspapers doing everything from reporting to photography and editing to website management; she won awards for her news and opinion writing in New York, Florida, and Maryland. She's also worked as an English teacher, a wedding videographer, a KMart cashier, a bookseller at Waldenbooks, a writer of press releases, and "the person that packs your Tupperware order," which was her very first job. She attended the Viable Paradise workshop in 2016 and the Clarion Writers' Workshop at UCSD in 2017.

Osborne lived in Albany for a while, near the Empire State Plaza, "which makes a cameo in *Engines*. It's an alien landscape to say the least." She currently lives in Baltimore, MD. Pre-pandemic, she played fiddle in the DC/MD-based Homespun Ceilidh Band, electric violin for a fusion outfit called Circle of Confusion, emceed the Charm City Spec reading series, and regularly ran 5k races. She is a full-time writer who lives with "two violins, an autoharp, five cameras, two cats, and a family."

What were some of the most important genre works for you when you were younger, and has your view of those books changed over time?

My one criteria for picking up a new book as a middle schooler was that it had a nice fat spine with a little rocket ship sticker at the bottom. That sticker led me to Elizabeth Moon's Paksenarrion books, Cherryh's *Cyteen* and *Downbelow Station*, to Sherwood Smith's Wren books, and to Lois McMaster Bujold's Vorkosigan series, all of which I still really like (and I kind of feel like I've grown up with Miles, honestly). I loved Gayle Greeno's trilogy about truth-telling alien psychic cats. The middle school library was also where I came across Brian Jacques' *Redwall*, a book that taught me that even the meekest of mice can defeat the worst of villains, which was a message I sorely needed to hear at that time in my life.

And then there are . . . the other books.

A lot of the novels I read then—books that were in the middle school library, that were actually recommended for us to read—normalized sexual violence and misogyny in a way that now makes me *extremely* queasy. I didn't notice it at the time because I was basically still young enough to believe in Santa. I can't read the Pern books anymore. I can't read Heinlein. I remember middle school as this time of growth where I really discovered how much I love reading and books, but when I go back to some of these older titles, all I see now is how much some of them *hated* their female characters. Hated them. *Fridged* them, objectified them, abused them.

And that's partially why I started writing. There wasn't a place in books like that for smart girls or ambitious women, but that's what I was and what I wanted to be. It was hard to find my cabin on the rocket ship, so I had to make one for myself. And that, right there, is the start of the journey for so many modern authors.

Did these books or stories have any measurable effect on your writing?

Absolutely. Artists are always working in conversation with the works they've consumed and the beliefs they had when they were younger, whether they want to interrogate those things or honor them. *Architects* actually reflects less on the books I read and more on the media I consumed, and wow, I consumed a lot of it. I grew up watching nineties science fiction television, which tended to see the world through rose-colored glasses, with protagonists who might have struggled but were generally on the side of the angels. That's partially why the explosion of space opera today is made up of more complicated narratives with protagonists who are less heroic and more human—most of the people showrunning *The Expanse* and the various new *Star Trek*s watched the same stuff as me, but it's been a long road since childhood, and our rose-colored glasses shattered a long time ago.

All of the shows I loved—the various *Treks, Stargate, Babylon 5*, and more—are basically utopiate workplace dramas, where the characters are extremely fulfilled both socially and vocationally, with found families and close friendships tied up in meaningful work. And, of course, that's not even close to how life is for most people. A lot of modern space operas acknowledge that people have realistic forces working in and around them, and that money and profit and power affect people on every level. So, yeah, I'm interested in black holes and space battles and Alcubierre drives, that's what I show up to the space opera bar for, but I'm also interested in how, for example, Ash Jackson balances her need to keep her head down in the corporate world with making a ruckus to save people, or how Natalie Chan decides how much of her soul to trade for the stability she's never had, or how much Leonard Downey uses humor as a survival tactic and what he's willing to give up for a chance at doing something real. In the real world you can't change things by walking through a stargate and shooting the nearest Goa'uld. It's a lot messier than that.

And it's that mess I'm much more interested in dealing with now.

You are also a musician. Are there important connections between your fiction and music, or are they very separate?

They are very much connected. Music is a language, just like English, and, as a musician, you interpret songs and symphonies in a similar way to how a writer interprets a paragraph or a story. I've found that pacing in music is uncannily close to pacing in story—simply listening to a song you like, where the music slows or swells, can help you figure out how a story might do the same. Intricate harmonies, crescendos, solos, and where they all go in a symphony—it's all directly applicable to what you do with words on the page.

And music is about the writing process, too, and the fandom that comes with it. Before the pandemic, I played the fiddle with a ceilidh band, which is all about dancing and fun and community-building. It's about trading energy with the rest of the band, relying on the beat, thrilling to the harmony, and trusting yourself and your fingers. It's meant to be danced to, it's meant to build community, it's meant to find people out of breath, hugging each other, laughing—or crying, or breaking open people's insides to find their deepest feelings. Music is also time travel—Dar Williams' "Iowa" kicks me straight back to 2001, while Gillian Welch's "Look At Miss Ohio" feels like Martha's Vineyard two weeks before the 2016 election.

I think we connect with books and fandom very much the same way. Reading is a quiet affair, but it shouldn't be a solitary one.

You went to both Viable Paradise and the Clarion workshop at UCSD. Did those programs have a significant impact on your writing or your career?

I tried for *years* to get into an MFA program, but the programs I wanted didn't want me, and when I got into Viable Paradise, I was *convinced* that I wasn't going to belong there. The workshop ended up being one of the most validating and encouraging experiences of my life. I came out of it with a bunch of close friends, some very encouraging words from actual professionals, and a critique group. That critique group has seen me through three novels, a handful of short stories, and a lot of related anxiety, and I'd argue, got me further than any MFA ever could.

Clarion pushed me. I learned something new about the craft every single day. My brain was on overload the entire time. We all were switched on so much that we'd take breaks from class and just lay in the grass, staring up at the sky. A lot of my classmates were honest-to-Jesus literary geniuses, whereas I came to San Diego worried that I couldn't keep up. My classmates and instructors pushed me to think about story in ways I never had before—kind of reached in and rewired it. That's how I explain it. I'm not sure I could replicate the process if I tried. (A lot of Clarionites say that you end up hearing your classmates' voices in your head while you're writing, and that's 100% true.) Two of my classmates ended up beta-reading *Engines of Oblivion* on literally a month's notice. An *entire novel.* That's what you do for other people when you've been through the Clarion crucible. I'll always be grateful for that.

Your Memory War duology is a foray into space opera. How do you define space opera, and what is the appeal of it for readers?

The term is originally based off of "soap opera," of course, but the genre hasn't relied on generic tropes and melodrama for some time. In fact, I think it's some of the most forward-thinking fiction being written today—because, in space opera, the only conventions by which you're limited are the fun, glittery ones. And those limits are *extremely* loose. You should probably have some wild political machinations, and some space battles, a neat-looking starship, and a laser sword or two, but other than that? The galaxy is your playground.

For me, space opera is a big, bright Broadway musical. It's full of squishy feelings and glitter and blood, and although people might not burst into song, that tingling, larger-than-life feeling you get when Lin-Manuel Miranda sings "Alexander Hamilton"…only on a galactic scale, with cool stuff liberally applied to everything and everyone. It's Enjolras stepping forward to start "Do You Hear The People Sing." *That's* space opera.

The genre is interested in the hard-SF questions of science and the galaxy and aliens and politics, but it's also interested in how all of those things affect human beings on the ground. How a spaceship works or how a technology functions is secondary to the political and personal ramifications. It's a massive grand strategy game, but also a very emotional and specific character-based RPG. Arkady Martine does it like nobody else in *A Memory Called Empire*—an entire empire's at stake, and it all depends on what one ambassador remembers. J.S. Dewes also captures the essence of space opera in the forthcoming *The Last Watch,* which is a bunch of military malcontents staring down the literal end of the universe.

Whatever you do, don't forget the cool stuff. Make it glitter. Make it glisten. Make it sing.

What was the journey like with Architects of Memory? Was it a project you started long ago, or did it start coming together more recently? Did the book change much from conception?

Architects is my own personal little katamari ball. The crew's been around since 1999, when I got really mad at a terrible movie and decided that I could do much better than that. I never really found a story for the crew I developed in my nerd rage, so into the round file they went.

In 2006, I broke my foot in five places and developed a blood clot that nearly killed me (and introduced me to the crap sandwich that is American health insurance). Turns out that I had a clotting disorder—which makes me uninsurable in American terms, and means that if the ACA is ever repealed and I get a blood clot, that's it, that's all, I'm done. Blood clots are awful, mentally and physically, and to get through the experience, I started joking about the clot as a "time bomb in my blood." I loved the phrase, but never thought up a plot that justified it, and into the round file it went.

The last card in the hand was dealt in 2015, when I moved to Baltimore and got churned up in the bloody teeth of the freelance gig market. By October, I was chewed to pieces making pennies on the dollar and just wanted to remember why I liked writing, so I decided to write a novel. (Yes, fellow writers. I hear you laughing at me. It seemed like a good idea at the time.) I was dinking around with ideas when I read an article where Elon Musk was talking about his company's desire to colonize Mars, and—I had just so many questions. That far out, Earth laws may be moot. Who's going to provide food, rent, water, and air? The company, of course, will have company stores with company prices, and we all know how that worked out in Harlan County. What happens if your boss on Mars is abusive? This is capitalism; the company's not there to help *you*. What happens when escape is three months and a billion dollars away? On top of that, when has colonization *ever* worked for anyone but the richest and most powerful?

The lesson is: Be an idea hoarder. Keep everything, even if it doesn't have a place when you think it up, because you never know when you're going to need it.

What were the most challenging aspects of writing Architects of Memory; and were the challenges very different for writing Engines of Oblivion?

Since I started *Architects of Memory* to have fun during National Novel Writing Month, pretty much, I didn't begin knowing where I wanted to go or what I wanted to do, so there were revisions—and more revisions, and even more revisions after that. I did so much writing. And it's not so easy when you're trying to write an alien species that is truly alien when you're bumbling around a human planet, as human as can be. Every single time I thought I truly knew the Vai or what they were about or how they lived, they whispered something different in my ear and it was back to the drawing board. I ended up dropping over eighty thousand words to get from the very first day to my final draft. That's nearly a novel in itself!

Engines of Oblivion was difficult, as well, but for a very different reason. I got to meander through writing *Architects of Memory*, to experiment and to dither. I'd just had my first child, and I was determined to make my deadline even though I was clocking somewhere around four hours or less of sleep per day. I was *seriously* sleep-deprived. I would keep my laptop close to me during the day, and when my daughter napped, I'd plunk her on my chest and write. Neither of them were ever more than six feet from my body. I wrote like this every day for months. I'd worked pretty hard before—freelancing can be a pretty abusive mistress—but this was an entirely different level. I probably won't ever work like that again, even though it ended up being an interesting experiment, and I kept quite a few of the gonzo ideas from Sleep Deprivation Land. Folks, always remember: You think writing is a mental game, but your mind is meat just like the rest of you. Take care of yourself. Don't be me!

***Architects* can be seen as a conversation on corporate power, capitalist class structure, healthcare, even the value of people. Is it important for fiction to take on these kinds of topics; is it an inevitable part of writing?**

It's absolutely inevitable. Space opera is social fiction that deals with systems and the effects those systems have on characters, and its emphasis on politics and galaxy-spanning drama means that even when a writer tries to just write "something fun," it's never just that. We often take the systems we live in for granted, but a writer never should. You have to think about systems to write space opera. We buy chicken at the market and don't think of the farmers or the packers. We pop tomatoes in our mouths without considering the farmworkers who have to wear long sleeves, even in the hundred-degree heat, because tomato plants can rip your arms to shreds. There were people in a Chinese electronics factory a couple years ago who committed suicide over horrible working conditions. Looking away from all of this is just as much of a political choice as getting involved, and that's true for writing, too. That choice shows up in your work.

Stories that don't acknowledge that these systems exist tend to ring false to me. Why do stories like *Star Wars*, which is the most binary good-and-evil tale in the space opera genre I can think of, still get so much attention? It's because the franchise spends a lot of time dealing with the question of who has power, who can get power, and what they do with it when they have it. Even the most bubblegum chick-lit romance deals with systems of power, chronicling the very real navigation of what it's like to be a woman in the world. If you don't deal with topics like these as a writer, you can't really drill into what your characters really believe as squelchy, real human beings, and that generally makes writing much blander than it could be.

Where does *Engines* take these conversations, and where does the story take the reader?

Engines of Oblivion takes us back into the central nexus of Auroran Company to follow Natalie Chan as she becomes a citizen and starts moving up the corporate ladder. It follows through on some of the plot threads set up in the first book, and takes you further into the crisis that ensues when human beings start poking around in alien weapons they don't quite understand.

Natalie finally has what she wants—citizenship—but the decisions she made in *Architects* are going to have consequences that will take her back to Tribulation and beyond. Natalie told a pretty big lie at the end of *Architects of Memory*, and lies reverberate—certainly for those she loves, and definitely for the whole galaxy, especially when the Vai return. Her bosses task her with finding Ash, the only person in the universe who must defeat them, and Natalie has to find Ash before their enemies do.

Engines also delves further into the issue of how memory makes us who we are. We've learned a little about how human memory interacts with Vai technology in *Architects*, and now we get to see how that plays out on a grander scale. Sometimes we can remember what we had for breakfast on a random day in January sixteen years ago, and sometimes we have entire years wiped from our memory—and sometimes traumas we block out consciously stay inside our cells, still informing our every move. Natalie has forgotten something—something that can build and destroy entire civilizations—and the Company wants it.

It's just as fast and wild and gross and complicated as *Architects*, and I give Natalie free rein to be her rebellious, striving, snarky self. It was a blast to write.

Some of the reviews on Architects praise not only inclusive representation, but the way it's pulled off: diverse characters as people organically inhabiting the story, living their lives, rather than feeling like a set of boxes are being checked. Was this a deliberate part of the reading experience, is this something that was carefully executed?

Thanks. It is really important to me to write fictional worlds that look like the one we actually live in—full of people of all origins and sizes and orientations and heights and classes and religions. Our world includes straight people and queer people and femmes and enbys, farmers who have never traveled more than ten miles from their village and people who qualify for multiple frequent flyer programs, and that's not going to change in the future. The only way to forget that our world is a wonderfully diverse place is to actively close your eyes against it. Many of the indentures in the company are climate refugees—Earth isn't doing so well—and if there's one thing true about the coming crisis, it's that it will touch literally everyone on the planet. It will be a truly worldwide disaster.

The characters of *Twenty-Five* have been the same since their inception—only their names have changed. For newer characters, I like to start with the setting, the world, and the culture, and work from there. Aurora started off as an international conglomerate built in the wake of war and climate change, and it names its ships after cities in which it has recruiting towers (and, thus, a big interest in the local economy). So, you see indentures from everywhere—Colombia, India, Canada, even upstate New York—and that was deliberate. Likewise, all kinds of gender expressions and sexual orientations are acceptable by Aurora, and Aurorans don't gender their clothing, and that was also deliberate. In this world, humans have learned some lessons. Some, but not all.

Many have also lauded the worldbuilding. What makes worldbuilding engaging for readers? Or, how do you write great worldbuilding? And what are some of your favorite worldbuilding elements in the second book?

On the page, I think good worldbuilding lives in the Goldilocks zone: not too little, not too much. Too much worldbuilding kills the sensawunda really good space opera needs for the reader. For example, I'm not interested in the science of midi-chlorians, but "the Force is unexplainable" makes me lose attention just as fast. You have to provide just enough information to the reader to keep them following the story, but not so much that they get bored or mired in detail.

Good worldbuilding goes "under the hood" just like the engine in a car. The reader might hear it, knows it's getting them from point A to point Z, but they don't see the pistons and the gaskets and the exhaust manifold. They're just enjoying the ride.

Engines was a worldbuilding dream. I really enjoyed pulling the trigger on things that I set up in the first volume, and it's full of (and I always imagine Oprah saying this) *consequences for everyone!* I cackled while writing *Engines*. A lot. There are some horribly delightful new Vai weapons. There's the memoria, a brain implant that's supposed to assist patients with dementia or memory loss in rebuilding their pasts. Natalie also has to deal with Ingest, a panopticon computer with some frightening secrets of its own. And there's the little Auroran social stuff that Natalie has to deal with this time that wasn't a problem on *Twenty-Five*—the list of unwritten rules she has to live by, the list of ways executives like Joseph Solano can get out of those rules (they are the 1%, after all), and the minute power dramas that are suddenly so important to everyone around Natalie. Now that she's on an executive flagship, everyone suddenly cares about who she's seen with, how her hair looks, and how loyal she is to the Board. And it's doubly stressful if a panopticon computer is feeding everything you do to the CEO.

Before the books launched you had some well-received short fiction out. What sorts of things did you learn about writing through the process of putting these books together? Will any of them impact the way you do short fiction?

Some authors can take breaks while writing their novels and write short fiction. That makes me incredibly jealous. I'm not like that. My brain very much prefers to stick to one project at a time, length be damned, so it's either a bunch of shorts in a row or a novel.

I mentioned before that the first book wasn't planned very well from the beginning and I had to kill a lot of darlings on its way to Tor—but that just taught me how to adapt. I didn't think I *could* plan—I always preferred the loosey-goosey pantsing methodologies of my earlier days that let me discover my characters and plots as I wrote. Well, it turns out that I love being a planner, especially now that I have a toddler that demands so much attention. I'm free to concentrate on words and structure and not worry so much about writing myself into a corner full of rabid plot bunnies.

And that is where short stories come in. I love plotting novels—and hate plotting shorts. Short stories let me be as experimental and wild as possible. They are chocolate. They are decadence. They are glitter. They are glorious things filled with the wild gonzo fancies that I love. They are short enough that I can write first and plan later, and scratch my pantsing itch.

And that's the most important thing I learned from writing these books: The best writing process is all about what works for you in the moment you're living in, and what works for you can change. Frustration with your process is just a warning that you need to give it a tune-up.

What excites you most about the duology, what do you really want readers to know about it beyond the blurbs and reviews?

Some people have used the word "dystopia" to describe the Memory War, but that's not entirely correct. The Auroran world is not a dystopia—or, it is, but in the same way our own society is a dystopia.

I often think "dystopia" is a word we use to lessen the blame we feel for how we affect our own world. After all, in dystopias, us common folk are all powerless drudges in gray outfits (except for the Chosen One, of course). So, there's no leadership to feel or power to reach for, and we can even abdicate our own responsibility, because what can people as small as us do about it?

We don't need a time bomb in our blood to understand that we do have power, even if we don't see it: over others, over our lives, over the things in our world that we can touch with our love and our influence. That's one thing people have told me about reading *Architects of Memory*—that it reminded them of that, and I was just so delighted to hear it. Ash and Kate and Natalie are yanked away from the world they hoped for to encounter the world as it actually is. And they step forward.

So, people can read this as a dark, lightning-fast space opera adventure story, and have a rollicking good time, and I'll be incredibly happy. But I also hope that readers come away from it thinking about their own universes, and where their priorities lie, and step forward, even if it's just a little. Because Elon Musk is going to Mars, and our climate is going to pot, and as I write this, the lines for food banks stretch six miles long in the richest country in the world, and we're all about to be Ash and Kate and Natalie.

What else are you working on, what else do you have coming up that new fans can look forward to?

I have a story coming out soon in *Don't Touch That,* an anthology about parenting in SFnal situations—it's about a teenage paladin, her mother, and a grand ol' serving of mom guilt, fried and festered over seventeen years and served fresh.

I'm also working on two new books. One's a space opera set in an entirely new setting, tackling questions of conservation and climate change and our responsibilities to the universe. A second is a fantasy novel based on a short story published in 2019, which is all lady gunslingers and internecine politics and a sorcerer on a hill. I also post new short and flash fiction from the Memory War universe on my Patreon once or twice a month for people who are interested in that, because there are still more stories to tell of the spacelanes between Europa and the White Line. I also yammer about *Star Trek* and writing on Twitter on a regular basis.

Thanks for speaking with me today; this has been delightful!

ABOUT THE AUTHOR

Arley Sorg is co-Editor-in-Chief at *Fantasy Magazine.* A 2014 Odyssey Writing Workshop graduate, he writes SF/F/H, reviews for *Cascadia Subduction Zone Magazine,* is senior editor at *Locus magazine,* and associate editor at *Lightspeed* and *Nightmare* magazines.

Science, Math, Fiction, and the Oxford Comma: A Conversation with S.B. Divya

ARLEY SORG

Born in Pondicherry, India, S.B. Divya moved to the US when she was five. She graduated high school in Minnesota, then did her undergrad at Caltech. Divya dabbled in one creative writing class during her sophomore year, but ultimately went for her computational neuroscience degree. She later earned a master's in signal processing from UC San Diego. From there she went to work as an electrical engineer.

Since her early teens, she attempted to write one story a year. In 2011 she tried her hand at NaNoWriMo, while also trying to manage home and work life, but fell a few thousand words short. The experience hurt, but the urge to write lingered, so she bounced back. In 2013 she took Gotham Writers Workshop's Science Fiction & Fantasy 1 class. In 2014 her first fiction sale, "Strange Attractors," came out at pro market *Daily Science Fiction*.

2015 was a big year: Divya took the Level 2 class at Gotham, started as a slush reader at *Escape Pod*, and had two more stories out, both at pro markets: "The Egg" at *Nature's Futures* and "Ships in the Night" at *Daily Science Fiction*. It was also the year she went to Condor in San Diego, her first SFF convention.

By 2016, Divya had a few short story sales and her novella, *Runtime*, hit the shelves, out with Tordotcom Publishing. She received an SFWA Nebula Award nomination for the novella and became coeditor of *Escape Pod* in 2017. In 2018 *Escape Pod* earned the first of two Hugo nominations for Best Semiprozine.

S.B. Divya, "Lover of science, math, fiction, and the Oxford comma," lives with her family in Southern California. She's been a DJ, an oil painter, and a mountain biker, and is into snowboarding, scuba diving, and more. She worked for twenty years as an electrical engineer in various fields, from machine intelligence to digital music. Her collection *Contingency Plans for the Apocalypse and Other Possible Situations* came out from Hachette India in 2019. *Machinehood* is her debut novel, due from Saga Press in March 2021.

What were the science fiction books that were important to you when you first started getting into science fiction, and do you feel like people should read them, and do they still hold up?

The most influential authors during my formative reading years were Joan D. Vinge, Frank Herbert, and C. J. Cherryh. The books of theirs whose spines I wore through were *Catspaw*, *Dune*, and *Cyteen*, respectively, though I read many of their other novels. When I was drafting *Machinehood*, I went back and read the opening chapters of each of them to study how those authors had set up their stories, and I was still impressed by the writing. I think all three would hold up pretty well in 2021, though there are modern criticisms that could certainly be applied to them. Given the new *Dune* movie coming out later this year, I suspect a whole new generation will discover the novel, too. I only hope that those people read the second and third books, which subvert some of the more problematic elements of the first one.

You've been coeditor at Escape Pod since 2017. Has editing had an impact on your writing? Does being a fiction writer give you a different editorial perspective from editors who aren't engaged in fiction writing?

I started as a slush reader at *Escape Pod* in 2015, and those years in the trenches definitely helped me improve my craft. Sitting in the editor seat has probably had less influence on skill, but it has given me emotional resiliency. Having to turn down other people's good stories helped me internalize that rejections, especially at the editor level, truly are a matter of taste and not an indictment about quality. On the flip side, being an author gives me more sympathy for what my fellow writers go through in the short story submissions process. I try to be forgiving of newer authors and their inadvertent mistakes when it comes to process or protocol.

Contingency Plans for the Apocalypse and Other Possible Situations came out in 2019. What was the process of putting together that collection?

The collection was a great experience! By sheer coincidence, when the editor at Hachette India reached out to me I was in Chennai for a family reunion. That meant that I could jump on the phone with her and not have to deal with the twelve-hour time difference. As someone who's struggled with bridging two cultures—I was in India until the age of five, and the USA since—I was thrilled to have my fiction introduced to my birth country. A lot of my stories incorporate some element of that duality, and the ones in the collection are no exception.

I suspect if the book had been assembled today rather than in 2019, we would've had some Zoom meetings, but as it was, we managed everything asynchronously via email. Promotion ended up being minimal and very pandemic-style, as well, since I was in California and couldn't attend in-person events. In spite of those challenges, I found the team in India to be very enthusiastic, responsive, and a pleasure to work with.

What, for you, are the top stories that you hope people will read in that book—the stories that you are most proud of, or that are most important to you?

The stories I'm proudest of are "Binaries," which packs a lot into a very small package; "Nava," which has some big far-future ideas that I love; "Microbiota and the Masses: A Love Story," which is set in Bangalore, uses lots of hard science, and is stylistically my homage to Tiptree; and "Contingency Plans for the Apocalypse," which I wrote in response to the political turmoil after the 2016 US election. All four are deeply geeky and science or tech heavy while also "punching you in the feels," as one of my readers said. If I had to describe my brand of fiction, that would sum it up.

You are an avid reader, a scientist, and a science fiction writer. Some people talk about science fiction as being a conversation, and science fiction authors often write books in conversation with or in response to other books. Do you see a relationship or conversation between your novel, Machinehood, and specific titles?

If anything, *Machinehood* is in conversation with pop culture and Hollywood depictions of artificial intelligence as well as biotech. Part of that comes from my educational background. Having a degree in a subject (in my case, computational neuroscience) makes it hard to accept unrealistic scenarios about that subject. In this novel, I tried to extrapolate from current technology to show what AI and cybernetics in our lives is likely to look like over the rest of this century. It's an alternative to the polarization in movies—either the very evil (*The Terminator*, *The Matrix*), or the very victimized (*A.I.*, *Ex Machina*).

In terms of books, I see this novel as something of a prequel or precursor to the story told in Annalee Newitz's novel, *Autonomous*. They cover very similar themes, but mine is set about half a century earlier, with less development having happened on various fronts, including AI. That said, I had already drafted my novel when I read *Autonomous*. I can't call my book a response to it, but I think they make for an interesting pairing.

Machinehood is your first novel out, but not your first book. Besides the collection and the recent Escape Pod anthology, you had a novella, Runtime, in 2016. Are there important differences in the structure, approach, or writing between the novella and Machinehood?

Short answer: Yes! Writing *Runtime*, which was on the shorter end of novella length, and required a vastly different skill set. I naïvely thought that writing a novel would be like writing a few novellas, but it's an entirely different experience. Writing a novel requires far more complexity of plot and character development. I especially learned my lesson that spending time outlining up front can pay a lot of dividends for long-form storytelling. *Machinehood* went through five or six major revisions before it went to publishers. In contrast, *Runtime* went through one. The novel I'm currently working on is based off extensive planning. I don't know yet if that means less time spent revising it, but I hope so.

One of the conceits of Machinehood is the way violence as entertainment meets gig economy culture, resulting in a system where body-guarding is partly about performance, and can be impacted in important ways by audience reaction. Is this a sly polemic against violence as entertainment? Is it a criticism of the direction of global economics? Or is it just a fun science fictional conceit, with no intentions around making any kind of statement?

It's definitely intended to make statements, both the polemical and the critical. It's also a commentary on our social media-obsessed culture. In the story, bodyguard work and the protests against corporate interests are funded largely by donations from the public, who can watch all the violence live via public drone swarms. I don't know if this will actually come to pass (I hope it doesn't), but it seems like a possible outgrowth from where we are today, especially if, as I imagine in the novel, we also develop biotechnology that makes it hard to do lasting physical harm to each other. I find that my favorite science fictional ideas sit squarely at the intersection of fun and meaningful. The former drives the plot, and the latter provides the story. At the end of the day, what I care about most—as both reader and writer—is how the conceit affects the characters, and it's hard to show that without making some kind of statement.

In your Analog interview you talked about coming back to the question of "what it means to be human" in your fiction. Are there important or specific ways in which Machinehood is the evolution of exploring this question through your work?

In this novel, I'm considering where the line is between biological and artificial people, and whether a line should be drawn at all. One of my frustrations with Western literature is how mired it is in dualistic thinking.

I prefer the continuum of Eastern philosophy, which I think meshes well with quantum physics and what is most probably the reality of our universe: That there are no hard boundaries in life. If so, what does that imply with regard to our treatment of different intelligent creatures? And how will we know when an artificial intelligence deserves equal treatment to a human being? Legal personhood has a long, complicated history, and the definitions and rights are continually evolving. At some point, we will have to examine complex intelligent machines and how they fit into our social and ethical framework.

Within a few chapters, there are a ton of science fictional ideas in Machinehood. Are there things in this book that readers might be surprised to find already exist, or things that are closer to happening than we might think?

Every technology in *Machinehood* is an outgrowth of something that's happening in current research. Some of it is very cutting edge and only exists in labs in rudimentary forms, but all of it is plausible. Of the ideas that might surprise people, I suspect that smart matter is one. I based that on these self-assembling M-Blocks from MIT. The "pills" in the novel, which are more like micromachines or nanomachines, are based on ideas like these tiny drug-delivery robots.

Some of the technological developments from the novel are happening faster than I expected, too. Networking constellations are one example. Elon Musk launched Starlink in 2019. It's not quite the same as what I envisioned for *Machinehood*, but it still took me by surprise. Drone swarms are also advancing faster than I'd anticipated. This is the peril of writing realistic near-future science fiction, but it's also part of the fun.

What was the journey to getting this book published—how did writing it start, what were the biggest challenges along the way, and what did you learn from the process?

Machinehood started out as a short story. After a couple rounds of failed rewrites—including one for a workshop—I realized that my problem was that this story was trying to span a novel's worth of content in five thousand words. The final product ended up drifting quite far from the initial concept, but everything has to start somewhere, right? I drafted the book in 2017 while not working a "day job," which was great because I'm a really slow writer. In 2018, as I embarked on revisions, I went back to work as an engineer. I also developed chronic migraines that year. Both of those factors slowed down my progress considerably. My biggest craft challenge along the way was the plot. *Machinehood* is a philosophical novel at its core, but has a thriller structure. I probably should've started with an easier subgenre! It worked out in the end, but if I had to do it again, I would spend more time figuring out the details of the twists and turns before I started writing.

Beyond the blurbs and reviews, what is the heart of this story for you, what do you really want readers to know about Machinehood?

This novel explicitly bridges the cultural divide that I mentioned earlier. It's the first time I've written a character (Nithya) who resembles the people in my family life. The romantic relationships in the book reflect my reality in Southern California—not only am I in a cross-cultural marriage, but many in my social circles are, too. The story moves around to places like Chennai and San Francisco, which mirrors the way I moved around as a child. My short stories have always had facets of me in them, but *Machinehood* is the first time I've captured so much of myself in one telling.

What else are you working on?

I'm hoping to have some new short stories published this year in various anthologies. They were originally slated to come out in 2020, but got postponed due to pandemic-related factors. Two of them are science fiction, and one is a fun little slipstream. I'm also working on a new novel set in the far future that's an epic space adventure. I love working with near-future speculative fiction, but I admit that it's been a nice break to spend time in a very different world, especially in 2020.

ABOUT THE AUTHOR

Arley Sorg is co-Editor-in-Chief at *Fantasy Magazine*. A 2014 Odyssey Writing Workshop graduate, he writes SF/F/H, reviews for *Cascadia Subduction Zone Magazine*, is senior editor at *Locus magazine*, and associate editor at *Lightspeed* and *Nightmare* magazines.

Editor's Desk: 2020 Reader's Poll Finalists

NEIL CLARKE

In late January, we held the first phase of our annual *Clarkesworld Magazine* Reader's Poll for best story and cover art. Maintaining the model we've used in recent years, the nomination phase took place online and lasted just under two days. The narrow window has continued to prove effective at minimizing the effects of ballot-stuffing and campaigning without having a significant impact on the participation level.

This year, it seemed clear from the start that a small group of works were destined to become finalists, but as the deadline approached the border blurred. At the buzzer, six stories tied for fifth place. Voters clearly felt passionately about these works, so it seems only fair to include them all as finalists, as a tie-breaker just didn't seem fair. They are worthy contenders, after all.

Without further ado, here are this year's finalists presented in alphabetical order:

Best Story

- "An Important Failure" by Rebecca Campbell
  (Novelette, August)
- "The Translator, at Low Tide" by Vajra Chandrasekera
  (Short Story, May)
- "Helicopter Story" by Isabel Fall
  (Novelette, January) Not currently available online.

- “One Time, a Reluctant Traveler” by A. T. Greenblatt
  (Short Story, July)
- “Distant Stars” by P H Lee
  (Short Story, April)
- “Lone Puppeteer of a Sleeping City” by Arula Ratnakar
  (Novelette, September)
- “Ask the Fireflies” by R. P. Sand
  (Novelette, September)
- “AirBody” by Sameem Siddiqui
  (Short Story, April)
- “To Sail the Black” by A.C. Wise
  (Novelette, November)
- “A Stick of Clay, in the Hands of God, is Infinite Potential”
  by JY Neon Yang
  (Novelette, May)

Best Cover Art

“Alien Scout” by Arjun Amky (November)

"Home Planet" by Beeple (April)

"Monk's Mirror" by Joseph Diaz (August)

"Family Portrait" by Yigit Koroglu (July)

"Ancient Stones" by Francesca Resta (October)

Congratulations to all our finalists!

Now it's up to you to pick the winner in each category. Go to:

www.surveymonkey.com/r/clarkesworld2020poll

And rank the stories by your order of preference. **Voting will close on February 15th at 8PM EST** and the winners will be announced in our March issue.

Speaking of awards, DisCon III—the 79th World Science Fiction Convention—has opened the nomination period for this year's Hugo Awards. Since there are still a few people who continue to nominate *Clarkesworld* for Best Semiprozine, I'd like to once again remind you that we haven't been eligible for that award for a long time. Give your nomination to one of the many fine semiprozines out there instead. You can find a list at semiprozine.org.

Beyond that, at present, there isn't a category for professional magazines, but you can nominate me for Best Editor Short Form if you are so moved, and of course, all our original fiction is eligible in their respective categories. The list of those works and the appropriate category for each story was included in last month's editorial at clarkesworldmagazine.com/clarke_01_21/. Our 2020 cover artists are also eligible in the Best Professional Artist category.

Speaking from experience, I can tell you that each little nod you give means a lot. Recognition doesn't pay the bills, but it has value, particularly after all everyone's been through in 2020.

Thank you and happy voting!

ABOUT THE AUTHOR

Neil Clarke is the editor of *Clarkesworld Magazine* and *Forever Magazine;* owner of Wyrm Publishing; and a eight-time Hugo Award Nominee for Best Editor (short form). His anthologies include *Upgraded, Galactic Empires, More Human Than Human, Touchable Unreality, The Final Frontier, Not One of Us, The Eagle has Landed,* and the Best Science Fiction of the Years series. His most recent anthology, *The Best Science Fiction of the Year: Volume 5,* was published in October by Night Shade Books. He currently lives in NJ with his wife and two sons.

Forward

COVER ART BY WENJUINN PNG

Wenjuinn Png is an independent artist and former graphic designer. He has provided illustrations for various game developers and his most notable works include the Panty Warriors and Bubblegum Space series.

Made in USA - Kendallville, IN
1232009_9781642360707
02.11.2021 0903